The Blood lie

A Novel

By
Shirley
Reva
Vernick

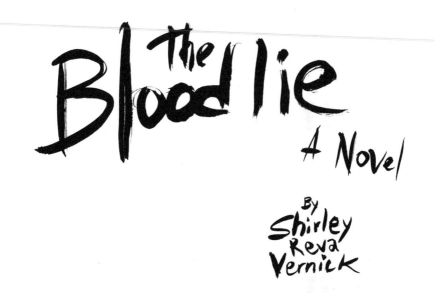

the Blood lie

A Novel

By
Shirley
Reva
Vernick

CINCO PUNTOS PRESS
www.cincopuntos.com

Printed in the United States.

The poem "Sorrow," by Edna St. Vincent Millay appears in *The Blood Lie.* From *Renascence and Other Poems* by Edna St. Vincent Millay (Harper, 1917).

First Edition
10 9 8 7 6 5 4 3 2 1

Library of Congress Cataloging-in-Publication Data

Vernick, Shirley Reva.
  The blood lie : a novel / by Shirley Reva Vernick. — 1st ed.
      p. cm.
  Summary: In 1928 in Massena, New York, Jewish sixteen-year-old Jack Pool, in love with his Christian neighbor, is accused of killling her little sister for a blood sacrifice.
  ISBN 978-1-933693-84-2 (alk. paper)
  [1. Antisemitism—Fiction. 2. Love—Fiction. 3. Jews—United States—Fiction. 4. New York (State)—History—20th century—Fiction.] I. Title.
  PZ7.V5974Bl 2011
  [Fic]—dc23

                              2011011429

Cover and book design by Antonio Castro H.

Many thanks to teen editor Hannah Hollandbyrd. *She loves this book!* And to good readers everywhere, especially Eve Tal and Lisa Sandlin. And to our friends in the Cinco Puntos Press West and East Coast offices for their support. You know who you are!

SATURDAY, SEPTEMBER 22, 1928

Jack Pool had been awake for a while already, but he waited in bed until the hallway clock chimed quarter past eight—the exact beginning of his sixteenth birthday. At least, that's what his birth certificate said. Earlier, the neighbor's mutt Agatha had snuck up on the Pool's chicken coop and gotten the hens squawking. If Jack were more like Harry, he'd have snoozed right through the racket, but he was a light sleeper. So he lay there, lightly humming, moving his fingers to his upcoming audition piece, and waited. When the clock finally rang the magic number, he slid off the bottom bunk, pulled his shirt and trousers onto his lean frame, and headed downstairs.

There was a light rap at the door. He opened it and found Emaline Durham standing on the front steps with her little sister Daisy. Emaline, the girl with the caramel hair and the voice like a flute. The girl he adored.

"Emaline, Daisy, hi," he said, pushing his black hair off his forehead. "Come on in."

"Hope we didn't wake you," Emaline said, smiling all the way up to her topaz eyes. "Your mother said it was all right for Daisy to come play this morning."

"Daisy?" came a little girl's voice from the kitchen.

"Martha!" Daisy took off.

Emaline moistened her lips and rocked gently on the balls of her feet. "Happy birthday, Jack. Wow, sixteen."

"Thanks. Yeah, can't wait to get my driver's license." For a split second, he imagined the two of them sitting close together in the front seat of the Pools' Model T.

"That will be great," Emaline said.

"What?"

"You driving, Jack. That will be great."

The image of them in the car disappeared. Driving would be fantastic, but driving with Emaline, that would never happen. Being casual friends with her was one thing. Being something more was something else. Impossible.

Emaline inhabited a different world from Jack's: the world of Christians. Normally, her orbit never would have intersected his. The only reason Jack and Emaline were friends, the only reason their younger sisters were playmates, was the miracle of their mothers' unlikely alliance.

The mothers had moved to Massena—and into Mittle's Boarding House—at the same time. They were both newlyweds, knowing no one except their husbands. The newcomers helped each other pass the days, with Eva Pool reading Jenna Durham the stories she was forever, almost obsessively, scribbling down—*there was so much to write about!* —and Jenna Durham playing her mandolin for Eva. Years later, when Emaline's father and uncle died in a car accident, it was Jack's mother who watched baby Daisy while the entire Sacred Heart congregation attended the double funeral.

"Do you get the day off for your birthday?" Emaline asked.

"Doubt it. We're taking delivery on a shipment today."

"Maybe I'll see you at the store then. Lydie and I are going shopping, so we'll probably stop by." She bit her lip, leaned toward his ear and whispered, "I was really hoping we could meet up in Paradise Woods so I could wish you happy birthday properly."

He could feel her breath on his neck. The blood rushed to his face in a hot wave. Over the summer, he and Emaline had twice managed to "bump into" each other on the path that cut through the local woods. The first time, they'd touched fingertips while they talked, flushed with anxiety over being caught. The second time, they'd gone behind a fat oak tree and almost kissed. Almost, because some men came trudging through on their way to work at the aluminum plant. Still, the thought of that kiss—and others he imagined—often kept Jack awake at night.

That was in August. When school started a few weeks later, George Lingstrom set his eye on Emaline. George—the captain of Jack's baseball team, the popular high school senior, the notorious flirt. Jack wondered if Emaline was interested in George. Why shouldn't she be? George was well-liked, good-looking. And Christian. That was that.

Jack groaned. "I'll probably be working late tonight," he said.

Emaline took a deep breath. "Rain check then?"

"Rain or shine."

"Good." She touched Jack on the sleeve, color spreading up along her cheeks, and then quickly turned and disappeared out the door.

"Someone here?" asked a drowsy voice from the top of the stairs.

Jack turned to find Harry, still in his nightshirt, plodding down the stairs. "Let's ankle it, pipsqueak," Jack said. "Go get ready for *shul*."

"Again?" Harry grumbled.

"Yup." They'd spent two full days in the synagogue last week for Rosh Hashanah, the New Year, and would be back again tomorrow for Yom Kippur, the Day of Atonement, but that didn't get them off the hook for the Sabbath. "And don't use up all the hot water," he added as he headed for the kitchen.

Martha and Daisy were sitting on the counter, watching his mother slice *challah* bread.

"Happy birthday, Jackie," the little girls chirped.

"Happy and healthy," added Mrs. Pool, a small, olive-toned woman with a single chestnut braid halfway down her back. She always wore her apron in the house, the one she made with the pocket big enough to accommodate a pad of paper and a few pencils. *Just in case of a story*, she always said. "Till a hundred and twenty."

"Are we gonna have a party?" Martha asked. "Daisy and me could make you a cake."

"No party this year, squirt," laughed Jack. He had much bigger plans than that. Plans for learning how to drive. Plans for getting a nickel-an-hour pay raise. And best of all, in three days, plans for interviewing at the Bentley School of Music in Syracuse.

Jack grabbed a piece of the sweet yellow bread and took a bottle of milk from the icebox. Eating over the sink, he silently recited the letter he'd memorized the moment it arrived last month:

Dear Mr. Jack Pool:

I am pleased to confirm your interview at the Bentley School of Music at four o'clock on Tuesday, September 25. Please bring your cello and your scholarship application with you. My office is located in Trumbull Hall.

Yours very truly,
Elihu Pierson, Dean of Students

Jack closed his eyes and tried to picture the elite boarding school—the classrooms, the auditorium, the dormitory, the musicians. He could hardly wait to go to the place where everyone loved music. A place where there were things to do. A place that wasn't this pit town of Massena, New York.

He felt a hand on his back. "Happy birthday, *shport*," said his father, his Yiddish accent shaping the last word into a cross between ship and port. Sam Pool was a short man with thick spectacles that hardly improved the poor eyesight he was born with. Blotting his graying mustache with a handkerchief, he added, "And a hundred more."

"Thanks, Pa...So, do I get the day off?"

Mrs. Pool jumped at this opportunity to make the point she made every Saturday morning. "Jack should always get *Shabbos* off. It's bad enough you break the Sabbath yourself, Sam. Do you have to encourage your son to do the same?"

"Friday is payday at the plant," he said. "Saturday is shopping day. I have no choice in it." He pointed toward his wife's apron pocket. "Some things can't wait, can they, my dear?" Turning toward Jack, he added, "I tell you what, *shport*. Tomorrow you can have off."

"We're closed Sundays, Pa," Jack said.

Mrs. Pool just rolled her eyes, then checked her hands for tell-tale pencil smudges.

———

The synagogue, a ten-minute walk from the Pools' house, was a small red brick building with tinted windows and heavy double doors. Jack, Harry and Mr. Pool climbed the front steps and entered the sanctuary, a simple room with twelve benches—six on the left for men and boys and six on the right for women and girls. On the *bima* stood a lectern and, against the far wall, a wooden cabinet that housed the two Torah scrolls. The windows spilled chartreuse light into the room.

"Where's Rabbi Abrams?" asked Harry, impatient for the services to begin and end. He fell into his usual spot, nearest the window in the second row.

"What difference does it make?" Jack asked, nodding to his friend Abe Goldberg. "We're only five yet." Ten men were required to hold a worship service, and they were only halfway there.

"Rats," Harry said. But by the time they put on their prayer shawls and *yarmulkes*, Rabbi Abrams was entering the sanctuary, flanked by a handful of other men. "Finally," Harry whispered.

Rabbi Louis Abrams was a compact man with a trim nut-brown beard and a scar on one cheek that turned into an S whenever he smiled, which was often. He nodded to the men and boys as he approached the *bima*, then took his place behind the lectern and began chanting the Hebrew prayers.

Jack grew restless within minutes. He'd felt restless a lot lately, stuck in this remote little whistle-stop that didn't even have a movie theater or a music store. Scarcely five miles from Ontario, Canada, Massena was locked between the St. Lawrence River on one side and the Adirondack Mountains on the other, a flat, bland expanse of nothingness. Most Massena men toiled as dairy farmers or laborers at the aluminum works, jobs they held all their lives and then passed on to their sons. People stayed on here—and so did their children—until no one seemed to notice the drudgery anymore.

No one except Jack. Every day he felt this place trying to

squeeze the music right out of him. No concert hall, no local quartet, no classical music on the radio. Jack didn't know what he'd do without Mr. Morse, who taught the skimpy school orchestra, gave lunch-period lessons, and, most importantly, spent untold hours with him after school, talking about fingering, bowing, rhythm, and the inner workings of the music. But Mr. Morse would be retiring at the end of the year. What then? What would he do then if he didn't get into the Bentley School?

Harry nudged Jack out of his reverie. "I saw Sarah gawking at you yesterday," he whispered.

"Huh? Sarah who?"

"Sarah Gelman, who else? Don't tell me you've never noticed her looking."

"Well, I haven't," he said, and it was the truth. How could Jack think about other girls when there was Emaline, the girl he'd almost kissed? The *only* girl he wanted to kiss.

"Don't you think she's pretty?"

Jack didn't hear him.

"Don't you?" Harry asked again.

"Don't I what?"

"Think she's pretty, genius."

"Yeah, she's okay."

"Want me to tell her brother next week?"

"No."

"Why not?"

Jack had nothing to say, so he said nothing.

"You think she's a bug-eyed Betty, don't you?" Harry said.

"I told you she's okay. I'm just not interested."

"How come?"

Rabbi Abrams saved Jack from Harry's inquisition by singing *Adon Olam*, the closing song. Harry had his shawl folded and put away before the hymn was over.

"Come, the store," Mr. Pool said to Jack. "Harry, your mother needs your help at home."

———

Pool's Dry Goods was one long room divided into departments by handwritten signs: SHOES. LADIES'. MEN'S SUITS & JACKETS. CHILDREN'S. HOME WARES. Roscoe, Mr. Pool's head clerk, was standing by the window, dressing the mannequins in work pants and boots. Other clerks were milling about the departments, chatting with browsers, folding clothes, and ringing up purchases.

"Who you rooting for today?" Jack asked Roscoe.

Roscoe took a straight pin from between his lips. "Yankees, 'course. You?"

"Any team with Lou Gehrig and the Babe is my team. It's the one good thing about having to work today—I can listen to the game on the radio here."

"You ain't got a radio at home?"

"Not on Saturdays. Got the delivery?"

"Shoulda been here half an hour ago. I'm just killing time. Why don't you...let's see..." He clicked his tongue, something he fell into when he was thinking. "How about you straighten up the men's pants?"

Jack frowned. "Got anything a little more interesting?"

"More interesting?" Roscoe blew a raspberry. "What you got in mind—cleaning the bathroom?"

Jack turned in resignation to the denims, figuring he'd

use the mental downtime to walk through his piece for the Bentley audition, but he stopped short when he heard a sweet and airy laugh nearby. He peeked around the pants rack to find Emaline and her older cousin Lydie sorting through the ladies' hat display.

In the sunlight, Emaline's eyes shone gold, and her ash-blonde hair reflected hints of red. Jack wondered what her hair smelled like today and decided on nutmeg or aniseed—something fresh and lively and a little exotic. She looked so beautiful to him that even her little flaws—the crowding of her teeth, the asymmetry of her eyebrows—made him feel crazy.

And her hands—what else had they touched today: her pillow, her skirt, her lips? Had they ever held another fellow's hand or felt anything close to the desire she inspired in him? From his hidden lookout behind the denim rack, he allowed himself to picture those exquisite fingers where he knew they'd never go. As that vision pulsed through his brain, he suddenly wished he weren't in public.

"Ooh, Em, I like the one you got there," said Lydie, a tall girl with round eyeglasses and a mouthful of Tutti-Frutti chewing gum.

Emaline tried on the wide-brimmed gold hat and studied her reflection in the wall mirror. "I don't think so," she said. "You try it."

"Not me," Lydie said, holding her hands up to her dark hair, which was cropped blunt and angular in the popular short style. "But here, try on this black one with the flower."

"Okay, help me with my hair, will you?" Lydie held Emaline's long curls high on her head while Emaline pulled on the bonnet.

Jack imagined that Emaline would pile her hair just like that when he took her to the school's fall festival dance next month. He pictured himself arriving at her front step wearing his best suit, the one he'd gotten for the Bentley School audition. *Her mother answers the door. Emaline's not right there. She's keeping me waiting while she slips into her heels. Then there she is at the top of the stairs, and it's like she floats down to my side. I have a corsage for her, white roses, and I pin it on the shoulder of her dress.*

It was one of Jack's favorite fantasies.

"Hey, Jackie," called a voice from behind. It was Roscoe.

Emaline glanced up. "Hi, Jack," she beamed. "Lydie, you remember Jack, don't you? It's his birthday today."

Lydie pushed her chewing gum against her cheek. "Happy birthday, Jack."

Jack had to force his eyes off of Emaline. "Hey, Lydie, it's been a while."

"From the looks of you, I'd say it's been at least three inches. How'd you get taller than me?"

"Listen, Jackie," Roscoe said, "the truck won't be here before one." Tongue-click. "You might as well go home till then."

"Hmm?" asked Jack. "Oh, right, I'll come back after lunch." Turning back to Lydie, he said, "I eat like a horse, that's how."

"Boys are so lucky that way," Emaline said. "They eat whatever they want, and it never goes out, just up." She smiled at his lanky frame, an unhurried, unselfconscious smile.

If only Jack had left for home right then, he'd have had that parting smile to keep him company. Instead, he helped Roscoe get a stubborn mannequin to stand up properly, and the extra five minutes was all it took for him to run into the last thing he wanted to see: George Lingstrom talking to

Emaline, eyeing her, laughing, standing too close, right there on the Main Street sidewalk.

Emaline was wearing the hat she'd just bought at Pool's Dry Goods—the black one with the silky red rose pinned to the side—and George was touching the flower in a way that brought the two of them nose to nose. Jack felt sick. *Is she flirting back at him?* he agonized. But no, he didn't really want to know, so he crossed the street and fled home, his fingers itching for the cello strings. Come January, with any luck, he and his instrument would move the 160 miles to Syracuse, and he wouldn't have to see George getting what he could never have.

———

When Jack got to the house, Martha and Daisy were clomping around the kitchen in Mrs. Pool's buttoned pumps and costume beads. Daisy had her face hidden behind a scarf, exposing only her golden eyes. They looked so much like Emaline's, he winced. Martha wore evening gloves up to her armpits and tripped on her too-long necklace.

"Careful now, girls," Mrs. Pool said without looking up from her writing. "Harry," she called out through the screen door, "how's the horseradish doing?"

"Almost done digging," he yelled from the backyard.

"What are you making?" Jack asked. He picked up a handful of the walnuts she'd just chopped before he realized he didn't have an appetite.

"Making ready for tomorrow's *shlug kapporus*," she said but kept on writing.

The *shlug kapporus* service took place every Yom Kippur eve in Rabbi Abrams' backyard. The rabbi took a live hen—

usually one of the Pools'—and held it over the congregants' heads while praying for the forgiveness of their sins. Then a few of the women cooked the bird in the rabbi's kitchen, preparing the meat to share with a needy family in town and using the bones to make soup for breaking the Yom Kippur fast.

This year the chicken meal would go to Frenchie LaRoux. It didn't matter that he wasn't Jewish; what mattered was that he needed it. People said he was so poor he didn't have electricity or a stick of furniture. When he won a used car at the Sacred Heart raffle over the summer, they claimed he just cut a hole through the wall of his shack and drove the car right inside so he could read by the headlights, sleep in the back seat, and warm his food on the engine. Regardless of where the truth ended and the tall tale began, Mrs. Pool clearly wanted the meal to be delicious.

"Jack," she said, pocketing her notepad, "I'm up to my ears in matzo balls. Take the girls out for a while, will you?"

Jack groaned. He wanted to be alone with his cello, to practice for his audition, to drown his thirst for Emaline in a sea of music. But it was useless to argue. Besides, watching Martha and Daisy for a while sure beat working in the kitchen. "How about a walk?" he asked the little girls.

"Downtown!" they shrieked at the same time.

"Just have Daisy home by noon," said Mrs. Pool. And so it was settled.

The girls held Jack's hands for a little while, but as soon as they rounded the corner onto Main Street, Martha and Daisy raced ahead to the confectionery shop. Crammed with penny suckers, licorice whips, saltwater taffy and all sorts of chocolates, the tiny store was a magnet for children. The girls pressed their noses against the window until it fogged up.

Jack stepped next door to the barbershop, where Walter Robinson displayed photos of the high school sports teams. Not that Jack was in any of the pictures—he wasn't, even though he'd been on the baseball team for two years now. He missed the photo shoots because they were taken at games. Games were played on Saturdays, and Mrs. Pool wouldn't hear of sports on the Sabbath (working on *Shabbos* was bad enough, she said, but at least that was out of necessity). Coach Romeo grumbled about it but let Jack work out with the team five afternoons a week—"because you can bat, dammit, and my outfield needs the practice"—even though he missed every game. He couldn't tell whether his teammates admired him or resented him.

Actually, he found out last spring how at least one of the guys felt about him. The team was in the common shower after practice when Moose Doyle called out in his larger-than-life voice, "Hey, Pool, were you born that way, or were you in a freak accident?" He wasn't pointing at Jack's crotch, but he might as well have been. Jack was the only circumcised boy on the team. Maybe he was the only circumcised boy Moose had ever seen.

Some of the other boys snickered. Some of them laughed out loud. Only when George Lingstrom told Moose to shut up did they all stop making noise. But they didn't stop staring. From that day on, Jack showered at home.

"C'mon," Jack said to the girls. "Let's keep moving."

They passed the apothecary, the jeweler's, J.J. Newbury's, the A&P and finally Pool's Dry Goods. "Can we go in, please, pretty please?" asked Martha. "I want to see Pa."

"He's busy," Jack said. "Let's cross the street instead."

He took the girls' hands and walked them across the road until they were standing in front of Gus' Sit Down Diner. The Sit Down was a shiny linoleum-and-Formica place that became the center of the universe early every morning and again at lunchtime. Sarah Gelman worked there part-time. *Maybe she's the one I should be pinning white roses on*, he thought. Sarah was likable and nice-looking, and, of course, she was Jewish, a fact that placed her within reach. But who was he fooling? Sarah wasn't Emaline and never could be.

"Who's that?" asked Daisy, pointing to a man emptying rubbish into a can in the diner parking lot.

"That's the owner," Jack said. "Gus." A squat, nearly bald man, Gus Poulos was chewing a cigar and trickling ashes every time he moved. "I eat supper here sometimes when I'm working late, and he brings me my food."

"His head's shiny," Daisy said, and Martha giggled. "Is he nice?"

"He's okay, I guess," Jack said. "He knows Mama goes to the Sunflower Café instead of to his place. And that's because the Sunflower makes pies and doughnuts for us—without lard. Gus would never do that. But he hates losing the business."

The noon bells from the Sacred Heart Church began to ring. "Okay. Time to get you home, Daisy."

"Aw," Martha pouted.

"C'mon," Jack said. "I've got to get back to the store soon, anyway."

As they headed back across Main Street and rounded the corner of Maple, it dawned on Jack that Emaline might be home when he dropped off Daisy. He couldn't face her—not right now. He knew *jealousy* was written all over his face, and he didn't want her to see it. So he dropped Daisy off at the foot of her driveway. He watched her until she disappeared inside, then challenged Martha to a race back home.

———

Emaline and Lydie cut through Paradise Woods on their way home. The dirt path was covered with end-of-year pine needles, and the leaves on the trees were already tinged yellow and red, but it felt more like summer than autumn. The woods ran on for miles, dense with scaly-trunked trees, spiky evergreens, jagged vines, and prickly shrubs, but if you stuck to the paths, there were some handy shortcuts, especially on a bright day like today.

"George Lingstrom sure thinks you're the bee's knees," Lydie said as they passed the boulder they called the Sausage Stone.

"Really?"

"Anyone can see he's goofy over you. And what about you, Em?"

"What about me?"

Lydie pushed her glasses up her nose and looped her arm through her cousin's. "Do you fancy him back?"

"Well..."

"Well what? The fall festival dance is coming up, isn't it, and I'll bet you dollars to doughnuts he's going to ask you. You'll say yes, won't you?"

"I suppose I will...I mean, yes. Probably. Yes, I'd love to go to the dance. With George. If he asks." It wasn't like Jack was going to ask her, after all. It wasn't like Jack could ask her.

"He'll ask."

"Hmm?"

"I said, he'll ask you."

"You know, his father's a drunk—at least, that's what Ma says, ever since he lost his job at the aluminum works. Cussing and hollering all day, and I hear—"

"But you're not going to the dance with the old man, are you?"

"Yeah...hey, do you have any ciggies on you?"

"Almost a full pack," Lydie said, stopping to spit out her gum. She pulled the box out of her coat pocket and lit one, handed it to Emaline, then lit another one for herself. "Let's duck behind that tree." She led Emaline to the same fat oak where Jack had held her hand.

"Mmm, that's good," Emaline said, taking a puff.

"Mother says they turn your teeth brown and your fingers yellow." Then she laughed. "She's such a worrywart."

Emaline leaned her head against the tree, exhaling a slow plume of smoke. "They remind me of Daddy, how he smelled like tobacco—tobacco and shaving cream. He smoked every night after supper and whenever we went driving. I wonder if he and your daddy were smoking when the accident happened. I wonder if the last thing they did in this life was take a puff of their Lucky Strikes."

"Couldn't say," Lydie said without much interest.

"You don't talk about him—about your daddy—much," Emaline said. "I probably talk about mine too much. Everything, everyone reminds me of him. Ma especially. She reminds me of him every time I see that look in her eye, that awful, sorrowful look. I don't know how you did it, you and your ma—you pulled yourselves together lickety-split."

Lydie let her ashes fall to the ground. "Maybe that's because—this is probably a terrible thing to say—but I don't really miss Father. I don't think Mother does, either. Oh, don't look so shocked. You know how he could be—his *spells*, as Mother called them. We never knew who was coming to dinner at night: the gloomy father, the mean and angry one, or the sweet one."

"I...oh."

"Don't tell me you never noticed."

"I guess so. It's just..."

"Just what?" Lydie asked, flicking her ashes on the ground.

"You know, denigrating the dead."

"That's the best time to denigrate someone—when they're dead. They don't get their feelings hurt that way. Honestly, I bit my tongue so often when he was alive, I'm lucky I can still talk. Ma and I are better off without him, and that's the truth."

Emaline tried to take a puff, but the smoke made her cough this time.

"Sorry," Lydie said, rubbing her cousin's back. "Sorry to spout off like that. Didn't mean to make you have a fit."

"I'm okay. I'm glad you told me. I should have figured it out for myself. It's just, you know, thinking about the accident and all...well...Ma wanted us home by 12:30 and it's past that now. We should go."

"Right."

Lydie and Emaline dropped their cigarettes and stamped them out with their feet. "Here, I have some Lifesavers," Lydie said. "Take one. Aunt Jenna will have a cow if she finds out what's been keeping us."

Mrs. Durham was heating a venison stew when the cousins walked in. "Finally," she said, pulling her hair back and leaning down to breathe in the gamey aroma. "Ah, that's perfect."

"I'm starving, Ma," Emaline said.

"Wash up and I'll get you some. Say, what's in the box?" She lifted the lid and examined the hat from different angles. A tall, statuesque redhead—people said she looked like President Coolidge's wife—she had a good eye for fashion and was always smartly dressed. "Very nice. Perfect for the autumn. By the way, Daisy was right behind you, wasn't she?"

"No," Emaline said.

"I just sent her out to call you. Told her you could all have lunch together. I thought that's why you came."

"We just got here, is all. Plus I'm famished."

"You must have crossed paths then. Well, she'll be along when she's done straggling."

Mrs. Durham sprinkled the stew with a medley of herbs and salt that she kept in an old milk bottle. She loved milk bottles and used them to hold everything from flowers to spices to the occasional pollywog. They were her closest connection to her Frank, who'd run the Sweet Creamery Dairy with his brother, and she kept them in every room.

She ladled out two bowls of stew and set them on the table. "All right, clean up after yourselves, girls. I have some bulbs to plant out front. I think I'll just give Daisy a shout first." She opened the back door and made a long, low whistle.

Gus Poulos was standing behind the register at the Sit Down Diner counting the dollar bills, while Sarah Gelman took inventory in the pantry and Tiny, the cook, stood over the deep-fryer.

"Twenty-three," Gus said to no one as he bit down on his cigar. "Twenty-three miserable little clams. And that's before you take out wages. For this I left Salonika?"

"You say something?" called Tiny.

"Yeah. I want you to tell me where to find the glittering gold roads and the marble sidewalks people told me about when I was a kid."

"Don't I know it?" Tiny said in his Irish brogue. "We all think we're going to live the life here, and we end up just barely getting by."

"Amen to that." Gus started to light a fresh cigar when the diner door jangled open and Roy Royman limped in. Royman hobbled to a stool at the counter and leaned his walking stick against the railing. "Morning," he said.

"You're late," Gus said.

"Hey, Tiny, whatcha cooking back there?"

"Shepherd's pie, meatloaf, doughnuts about to come out of the fryer. You want?"

"Any hash browns left?"

Tiny shook his head.

"Eh, give me a slab of meatloaf, and save me a couple doughnuts, plain."

Gus led Royman to the table nearest the noisy window fan.

"We on for tonight?" Royman asked.

"Rum boat'll be here between midnight and two, depending."

"Depending on what?"

Gus shrugged. "Depending on everything. Anyhow, get the truck here by eleven-thirty."

"Why's it got to be so late, that's what I don't understand," Royman said. "What am I supposed to tell the missus?"

"My Bettina just thinks I'm out gin milling. Anyway, let's make it eleven straight up, just to be sure."

"Yeah, yeah, whatever you say."

Gus and Royman's smuggling operation was easy money during these Prohibition days. Whiskey and wine were legal a scant mile across the St. Lawrence River in Canada. All it took was knowing one Canadian with a boat who was willing to load up with alcohol and meet you somewhere. Then you let a few discreet friends know you had a supply. You might let the Mr. Lingstrom-types know, too. You might even let a Jew know because the Jews used wine to welcome the Sabbath, and if you couldn't get business from the sheenies on your pies and meats, you might as well get them with the hooch.

Better yet, you kept your direct dealings to a few trusted customers, and let them sell their stuff to the Jews and the drunks.

Tiny appeared with a plate heaped with meat and biscuits. "Doughnuts'll be another minute," he told Royman.

"Anyways, I gotta work," Gus said as the first paying lunch customer strolled in.

When Lydie and Emaline finished their stew, they settled into the living room to do some beading. Emaline was finishing up the bracelet she was making for her mother's birthday next month. Lydie decided to try her hand at a choker.

After a while, Mrs. Durham came in from the garden and walked over to the telephone. "It's 1:30," she said. She picked up the receiver, then put it down, hesitated, then picked it up again. Finally she spoke to the operator. "Good afternoon, Bess. Would you put me through to my sister-in-law? Thank you."

"Clarisse?" Mrs. Durham said after a moment. "Yes, Lydie's right here. She can stay as long as she likes. Listen, Daisy didn't happen to walk over there, did she?...No, everything's fine. Maybe she wandered back over to the Pools' house...Yes, I do trust that family, Clarisse...Yes, I know them well enough—Eva Pool is my friend...No, nothing else. I'm positive, Clarisse."

Next, Mrs. Durham tried phoning the Pools, but no one answered. Then she called her cousin Mickey and the Pikes down the street, whose new litter of barn kittens drew the neighborhood children, but they hadn't seen her. She called the Pools once more, again with no luck.

"Emaline," Mrs. Durham called.

"Yeah?"

"Daisy must still be in the woods. Go fetch her, will you, before that stew spoils? Both of you."

"Can we finish our beading first?"

"No," she said more sternly than she meant to.

"Okay. Come on, Lydie."

Mrs. Durham handed Emaline a biscuit in a paper bag. "Here," she said. "Give this to her right off. She'll be half-starved by now. And keep at it till you find her, you hear? I'll whistle for you if she beats you home."

———

After Emaline and Lydie had hiked the forest path for a little while, chatting and calling for Daisy every now and then, Lydie put a fresh piece of gum in her mouth and said carefully, "Your mother seems pretty upset."

"She's always upset," Emaline said. "Upset and worried. Like I said, we haven't pulled ourselves together like you and your ma have. She's just overreacting. Honestly, how far could Daisy have gone? She's only four year old! She's probably poking around for frogs or stones, the way she always does."

"Daisy?" Lydie shouted.

Another half-hour passed.

"*Little girl, little girl, where have you been? Gathering roses to give to the Queen,*" said Emaline. "*Little girl, little girl, what gave she you? She gave me a diamond as big as my shoe.* Daisy?"

"C'mon, Daisy, we've got a biscuit for you," Lydie called. Her voice was getting scratchy. "What time is it, anyway? It gets dark so early this time of year."

"It's...*God!* It's going on four. I had no idea. She's been out here since—when did Ma say she sent her out?"

"I don't know. Hey, do you see any deer traps?"

"Oh, no," Emaline moaned. "*Boys and girls come out to play, the moon does shine as bright as day. Come with a hoop, and come with a call, come with a good will or not at all...* Daisy!"

The girls walked on until they were dragging. "Are your feet hurting as much as mine?" Lydie asked.

"They're burning," Emaline said. "I'd love to dip them in the river about now...the river! Ma never lets her near the water alone, it's so cold, and the undertows and the drop-offs, what if she accidentally...?"

"No one jumps into the river by accident, Em, not even a little kid. Calm down. You either jump or you don't, and she knows better...hey, listen."

"What?"

"*Shhh*. Listen. Over there, I think, in the brambles. Footsteps."

"Daisy? Daisy?" Emaline called. Twigs and leaves crackled underfoot, but no one answered. "Daisy?"

A raccoon waddled out into the open. It rubbed one eye and swished its plump tail, blinked, and scooted back into the brush.

"If I'd just gone straight home like I promised," Emaline said. "If only I'd been on time. If only..."

"Look, maybe Daisy's already home," Lydie said. "Maybe your ma whistled for us but we were too far away to hear. Maybe that's why we can't find her."

"So should we —?" She straightened abruptly. "Lydie, listen. I hear something...Daisy?"

"Nope, just us," came a man's voice. Emaline's neighbor Jed Pike and his son Emmett stepped out from a crowd of evergreens. "Your mother called us about Daisy. Afraid we haven't had any luck so far."

Emaline stole an anxious glance at Lydie.

"Don't you fret now," Mr. Pike said, stepping closer. He

smelled like cows and hay. "My nephew is out here too, and your mother had an alert put on the radio, so there'll be others. We'll find her. Say, you ladies have lights?"

"Lights?" Emaline said. "No. We didn't think we'd be out this long. We thought we were just—"

"You might want to get something then," he said. "The sun'll set in another hour."

The girls stared at him.

"Good idea," Lydie finally said. "C'mon, Em, let's scoot back to your house for a flashlight or a lantern." She tugged at her cousin's arm until Emaline finally let herself be pulled along.

———

When they got to the house, Emaline couldn't find her mother—the house was so crowded with neighbors and friends. "What are all these people doing here?" Emaline asked Lydie. "Look at all the food they brought, like for a funeral." She looked around for Jack, but he didn't seem to be here. Maybe he was out looking for Daisy.

"Why is everyone staring—?" Emaline said. She stopped mid-question, her legs suddenly wobbling, her head light.

Lydie helped her onto the sofa. "Let me get you some water," she said, lifting Emaline's feet onto the coffee table. "Or some juice. You need something—I'll fix you a plate."

"No, I'd gag on it." She leaned her head against the sofa and closed her eyes. "I'm fine, I just need a minute. Just one minute."

"Miss Durham?" came a deep voice overhead. "Emaline Durham?"

Emaline looked up to see her Aunt Clarisse and a uniformed man hovering on the opposite side of the coffee table.

"Emaline," said the big man with the brick-red mustache. "I'm Victor Brown, state trooper, and I want you to know—"

"I've seen the trooper. He's older than you. And a lot shorter."

"That was Billy Moore." He said the old trooper's last name like it was MOO-wah, like it had no 'r' in it, like he wasn't from around here. "He left a few weeks ago. I'm your trooper now. I'm in charge of this case."

"Case?

"Case. Your aunt wants me to tell you—"

"Where's my mother?" Emaline took her feet off the table and started to stand, but Lydie pulled her back down.

"In the kitchen, dear," Clarisse said, taking a seat on the sofa and squeezing Emaline's hand with her pudgy one. "She really wants to see you."

"Well, what the heck does he want?"

"I just—your aunt wants you to know we got a lotta men searching for your sister," the trooper said, twisting one end of his mustache between his fingers. "Upwards of a hundred, by my last count, including the whole fire squad. Won't be long now till we get her home, I think. Anyways, you should call it a night, miss. It's getting dark. No time for a young lady to be out."

"You're right," she said. "It's no time at all for a *young lady* to be out. So we'd best get Daisy *in*, hadn't we? Now if you'll excuse me, sir, I'm going to go find my sister."

"I'm gonna insist now, miss," he said. "We don't need two girls going missing on us tonight."

Emaline shot him an acid glare, then stood up and headed for the kitchen. As she went, she glanced at the mantelpiece clock. It was past six. Daisy had been missing since lunchtime—*six hours!*—and there still wasn't a sign of her. She'd vanished, and no one knew where or how.

———

Mrs. Durham sat at the kitchen table, her chin on her hand. She was surrounded by a flock of women who stepped aside as soon as Emaline came in. The choir teacher and Sister Frances were there. So were most of Mrs. Durham's quilting bee ladies, all of them with grim, pressed lips and narrow eyes.

"The poor dear," one of the women whispered. "First her father and now this." Did she really think Emaline couldn't hear her?

"Ma?" she said, stepping closer.

When Mrs. Durham raised her chin, Emaline let out a small gasp. Her mother looked just like one of the mannequins at Pool's Dry Goods—so stiff and pale, staring at nothing.

"Emaline, thank heavens you're all right," she said. "I was getting worried about you too."

"I couldn't find her, Ma. But I will. I'm going to find her."

"No, stay inside. I don't want you wandering those woods at night."

The other women murmured their agreement.

"I have to, Ma."

"But...," She squeezed Emaline's hands. "Just be careful then, do you hear me? Be careful. Promise."

"I promise. I'll be back as soon as I can, honest." She glanced at the women, then back at her mother. Then she left the kitchen without saying good-bye or thank you or any other thing to anybody.

Lydie was waiting for her by the coffee table. "How's your mother?" she asked.

"She looks just like she did the day Daddy died. Like a shell, like a broken shell."

"I'm sorry, Em."

"Yeah." She scanned the room again and cleared her throat. "What's going on out here?"

"Nothing but bull. Spud McMann is beating his gums about hungry bears walking down the middle of the street over in Potsdam. Mae Petru is yammering about the maximum-security prison in Dannemora, how it's only an hour away, how she wonders if they ever escape. I blocked out the rest."

Emaline's eyes started to glisten.

"Come on, Em, they're all just a bunch of saps, gossiping instead of doing something useful. Look, I found a flashlight in the other room. Let's head back out." She took her cousin's hand and gave it a tug.

Emaline took a shaky breath, then the two of them hurried out the door where the first stars were twinkling in the evening sky.

———

Pool's Dry Goods was closed for the night at half past six, but Jack, Mr. Pool and Roscoe were still there. Roscoe and Jack had been in the backroom all day unloading the winter clothes shipment and listening to the Yankees-White Sox game on the Canton radio station. Now Jack was sweeping the front walk and rolling up the window awnings while Roscoe collapsed shipping boxes for the rubbish.

"Jack," Mr. Pool called out the open door, "that's all for one day. Here, take this and eat at the diner, save your mother from cooking another meal."

"Okay." He took the dollar from his father. "I'll have change for you."

"Keep it. For your birthday."

"Thanks, Pa. You coming home soon?"

"After a while."

'Night, Roscoe. Who's going to win tomorrow?"

Roscoe clicked his tongue. "Indians."

"Not a chance, not against the Yankees. See you next week."

———

The Sit Down Diner was busier than usual tonight. Old Man Claghorn had dropped in for a slice of pie on his way home from the aluminum works. Bucky Sanborn, the traveling paper salesman, was there, and so was Frenchie LaRoux, who didn't order anything but was chatting with his table neighbors—Dr. McCarthy on one side and the Lorado brothers on the other.

Chuck Petru was eating home fries at the counter, reading the *Observer* and waiting for his wife to show up. At the other end of the counter, Roy Royman nursed a cup of coffee while Gus wiped down the doughnut case with a dishrag.

Gus had heard about Daisy's disappearance from Tiny, who'd heard the afternoon radio announcement—*WMSA is asking folks to keep a lookout for four-year-old Daisy Durham, daughter of Jenna and the late Frank Durham, who entered Paradise Woods off of Ransom Avenue shortly before one o'clock today and hasn't been seen since. Mrs. Durham asks for volunteers to help search the woods for her daughter.*

Gus had scowled when he learned the news but said nothing. An hour later, when his wife stopped by on her way to bring pierogies to Mrs. Durham, he got a little edgy. Finally, when Roy Royman came to say the trooper had ordered the whole fire squad to search the woods and the river, Gus blew up.

"We've got a date with a whiskey boat smack dab in the middle of a missing-person search," he hissed at Royman. "What if that greenhorn trooper sees and decides to get patriotic on us?"

"You giving him free meals like you did Billy Moore?" Royman asked.

"Coffee and Danish nearly every morning, but we can't bank on that."

When the diner door rattled open for Jack, Gus and Royman were the only ones who looked up. The closer Jack got to the counter, the quieter Gus spoke, until he finally stopped himself mid-sentence.

"Get you something?" Gus asked.

"Scrambled eggs and toast, please," Jack said. It was all he ever ordered, the meats, pies and pastries not being kosher.

Gus wrote down the order and handed it to Tiny at the grill. "You're working late tonight, boy," he said to Jack.

"Hmm? Oh, we had a shipment to unload. Plus we'll be closed Monday for our holy day."

"Holiday? Which one?"

"Yom Kippur."

"Yom Kippur." Gus let the words roll around on his tongue. "That the one where you light candles for a week?"

"No, that's Hanukkah. In December."

"Right. Hmm. Well, your order'll be right up."

When Gus went back to his spot opposite Roy, Jack disappeared inside his own thoughts: *Do I really have a shot at getting into the Bentley School? Mr. Morse thinks so—he thinks I have real talent. I'm going to spend the whole evening practicing my audition piece. I wonder what Emaline will be doing tonight. What were George and Emaline talking about on the sidewalk today, anyway—was he asking her to the fall festival dance?*

Old Man Claghorn plunked his dirty plate on the counter and brushed piecrust crumbs off his shirt with Gus' wiping towel. "So long, all," he said, patting Chuck Petru on the back.

"Not too long," Gus said. "We've got coconut cream pie coming up tomorrow." His gaze slid over to Jack for a moment. "Rhubarb, as well. Nice flaky crusts, guaranteed."

The door no sooner clattered behind Old Man Claghorn than Bud Carbino, the jeweler, walked in with his poker mates. Gus dropped a plate of eggs in front of Jack and went to greet the newcomers.

———

Emaline and Lydie pressed on through the black snarl of trees that was Paradise Woods after dark, listening to the Sacred Heart bells ring seven times.

"Everything looks the same," Emaline said, swinging her flashlight this way and that. "Every tree, every rock. No wonder she got lost."

"Daisy!" Lydie called out. "Daisy, remember this one? *Croak, said the toad, I'm hungry, I think. Today I've had nothing to eat or to drink. I'll crawl to a garden and jump through the pales, and there I'll dine nicely on slugs and on snails.*"

A bullfrog answered with a low, scraping tone, but no Daisy.

"You know what I wish?" Emaline asked. "I wish I could turn back the clock and get home from shopping on time— early even. Then Daisy would never need to come out here to call us. We'd all be sitting around playing board games right now. God, I wish."

Lydie cracked her gum loudly. "I see flashlights in the distance up there. With any luck, you'll be taking the checkers board out yet tonight."

Emaline squinted in the direction of the lights. "How many you think there are? The trooper said something about a hundred men, but it looks pretty sparse to me."

"Maybe the rest are hunting somewhere else."

"Or maybe they got tired and went home."

Lydie didn't respond.

"Too bad the old trooper isn't around any more," Emaline went on. "They say he really knew his onions."

"Mmm."

"Lydie?"

"Uh huh?"

"Back home, did you happen to notice...did you see anyone our age?"

Lydie lifted her skirt as she stepped over a fallen branch. "You mean George Lingstrom?"

"No, he told me he was going fishing at his uncle's in Norwood today. I just meant...anyone else."

"I saw Margie Helmer right when we walked in. That's all I can remember. Why?"

"I'm just wondering where my friends are. I wonder if they're out searching."

"Maybe. But maybe they don't even know. If they didn't have the radio on or—"

"Everybody knows about this," Emaline snapped. "Everybody! What I want to know is, who's doing anything about it?"

"I only meant—"

"Never mind, forget I asked," Emaline said. "Let's just keep going."

———

Gus still had his diner apron on when he got to the Durham's a little after 7:30. He caught sight of his wife and quickly untied it.

"Gus?" said Bettina. "Who's watching the diner?"

"No one. Tiny. I just wanted to see what's going on. And to get you home."

"No, the quilting circle is all staying. I'll get myself home. You'll manage without me—I left a dish of cannoli in the icebox for you."

"I'll be late tonight, myself."

Bettina frowned. "You aren't going *out* on a night like tonight?"

"Hush your voice. I'm not going *out*. I'm just...going to keep the diner open late on account of the search. Men'll be getting cold and hungry out there, maybe wanting some coffee and pie."

"Well! That's real neighborly. You go on, then."

"Okay. See you later." He squeezed her arm and started toward the living room.

"Gus? I thought you were going back to the diner. I don't know if Tiny can do it alone."

"He'll be fine for a few more minutes. I need to talk to that trooper first. I have an idea—a lead."

"About Daisy?"

"Maybe."

"Why, Gus, what on God's green earth is it?"

"I'll tell you more when I get home. Don't you worry. Everything is going to be fine. Now, where's the trooper—is he here?"

"In the dining room, last I saw," Bettina said, giving him a victorious little kiss on the cheek. "I'm off to wash dishes. You go solve the case for the trooper."

———

When Jack got home from the diner, the house was so still he wondered if his family had gone out. But then Mrs. Pool called from the dining room, "Jack? Come, we're just starting." It was time for the *havdalah* blessing, which marked the end of the Sabbath, and she, Harry, and Martha were already gathered around the dining table. Jack rubbed his tired eyes and joined them.

The *havdalah* candle was really two candles twisted around and around each other like a braid. One wick stood for the Sabbath; the other, for the ordinary days. Mrs. Pool touched a match to both wicks, and when their flames joined together, she said, "Here we leave the Sabbath and start the week renewed." Then she doused the candle so she could reuse it next week.

That's when Jack realized his birthday was almost over. *Some special day this has been*, he thought.

"Can I have the salmon box first?" Martha asked.

"*B'samim* box," Harry corrected her.

"Well, can I have it first this time?"

Mrs. Pool handed her the small silver box filled with cloves and cinnamon and studded with diamond-shaped holes. Martha shook the box and held it to her nose, inhaling so deeply she coughed. "Mmm, that smells soooo good," she said and passed the box on.

Smelling good was the whole purpose of the spice box. According to Mr. Pool, it was meant to cheer people up when they were feeling sad that *Shabbos* was over. Mrs. Pool said it was supposed to remind everyone to carry the sweetness of the Sabbath into the week. When the box made its way to Jack, he lingered over the sweet and peppery aroma, imagining it was Emaline's hair. One breath of the spices and he was dancing with her at the fall festival dance. One more breath and he had to put away the box for another week.

"Come along, Martha," Mrs. Pool said, taking the good cloth off the dining table and folding it. "We'll check on the chickens before we make the almond bread."

"I'll check on them, Mama," Harry volunteered. Anything not to be sent back to kitchen duty.

"Fine." She laid the linens aside. "Jack, you can peel that basket of potatoes sitting in the sink."

"Can't I practice a little first—for just a few minutes?" he asked.

Jack could feel Harry bracing to protest if their mother caved to Jack. So when she winked her okay, he raced upstairs before Harry could open his mouth.

"So what's all the secrecy?" Victor asked once he and Gus got into the police car in front of the Durham's house.

"I'll tell you flat out," Gus said. "It's time you knew. This girl who disappeared, it's the Jews." His lips curled as if the very word tasted bitter.

"The Jews?"

"They have strange customs for their holidays. Terrible customs. They use blood. Drink it and bake it in their special foods. Blood of a Christian child, not one of their own. One of their big holidays is in a couple days, see. They call it Yon Kippur or something. That's why they took Daisy. I just hope they didn't murder her yet, that they're holding onto her till their big day. If you move fast enough, you might save her."

Victor's eyes narrowed, and he started twiddling his mustache. "What makes you so sure about this?"

"One of them Jews came into the diner a few minutes ago and couldn't keep his mouth shut. Kept dropping hints. Like he felt guilty and needed to talk. I put two and two together, that's all."

Victor gripped the steering wheel.

"Stop futzing with them woods for a kid who isn't even there," Gus persisted. "Listen to me. I'm telling you the truth. I know what goes on in this town—I hear everything every day at the diner. It's those Jews that—"

"*God*—" Victor muttered, shaking his head.

"Wha' you say? You know something?"

"I know what I've seen. I know my pap used to make

good dough selling groceries. Had his own storefront on the East side of Buffalo. Then the kikes moved in. Set up shops all along Main Street. Kept jewing down the price of things, smiling all the while, till my poor pap couldn't make a living, couldn't even make rent on the joint. Landlord gave him the bum's rush. Just like that, out on the street, all on account of those bohunks. Been driving a bus ever since."

"Might've been the sheeny curse, to boot," Gus said. "I hear if they raise their skullcap at you, it unleashes the curse, the curse of going flat broke. Maybe that happened to your pap."

"It was right around this same time of year," Victor went on. "Yeah, right around this same time, 'cause I was just starting at St. Agnes Academy for Boys by then—autumn. We got to school one morning, found out the chapel was broke into the night before. And what do you suppose was missing— the fancy candleholders or the pricey linens? No, the host, that's what. Those dirty Jews stole the host!"

"Sick, just plain sick."

"Hell, it don't seem like nothing compared to this. *Jeezus*, human sacrifice, in this modern day and age...but—you know, the widow Durham, she thinks the girl just lost her way in the woods."

"That's hooey. She's not thinking straight."

"So, this Jew you talked to, this—what'd you say the man's name is?"

"It's a kid. His name is Pool. Jack Pool, Pool's Dry Goods," Gus said.

"Did he say where they got her?"

"Couldn't get that much out of him. But listen, their stores are already closed for the holiday, locked up, black as night.

Wouldn't you say that was convenient if you have a child—or her body—to hide?"

Victor turned the steering wheel as far as it would go in both directions, then sat back into his seat, rubbing the wiry hairs of his mustache. "Okay, look, tell me *exactly* what this kid said."

Gus licked his lips, thinking about the whiskey coming his way, about how it would tingle in his mouth and burn his throat tonight when he toasted his latest stash with Royman.

"Well, the diner was slow tonight—probably because everyone was out hunting for Daisy. I was thinking about closing up early but decided to stay open and give out coffee and pie to the search parties. So there I was, standing at the counter talking to Roy Royman about how they couldn't find the poor little girl—this was no more than an hour ago—and in walks this Jack Pool. Jack scrambled-eggs-and-toast Pool. Orders it every time. Never a real meal. It's the Jew way, see. They won't eat any meat their preacher doesn't kill personally. Now Chuck Smith—he runs the Sunflower—he makes them Jew-pies using Crisco for shortening. I hear he even plays pinochle with them, lets them—"

"So—?"

"Right. Anyways, when Jack bellies up to the counter tonight, I chat with him, see, being friendly like I am with all my customers. 'What's new?' I ask him. That's when he tells me about this holiday of theirs coming up. I get him his silverware and a glass of water. 'You hear about the Durham girl?' I say. He doesn't say a word, but goes pale as a sheet. Then he starts twisting his napkin over and over like he's strangling it. And right then, that's when I remembered something my grandmother in Salonika used to tell me. Every time I'd leave the house, she'd warn me, 'Watch where you walk. Them Jews are all born blind and need blood to be able to see.' The Pool boy, his father is blind—you follow? So it was all beginning to make sense to me. You see how it makes sense?"

Victor took a deep breath and rubbed his eyes. He nodded slowly.

"You ever dealt with a missing child before?" Gus asked.

"Nope."

"Bet the big guys at HQ'd think you're the cat's pajamas if you solved this one."

"Or a chump if I botch it."

"Then here's the part you really need to understand, Victor." He fingered the fresh cigar in his pocket. "These Jews always leave the body where people will find it and be afraid. So even if Daisy's already dead, she's not under some rock in the middle of the woods. They're gonna do whatever they're gonna do to her, and then, after their holiday's done, they're gonna dump her somewhere obvious. And you're gonna look like a fool for not noticing her there, guaranteed."

"*Jeezus!* Looks like Billy Moore got out of this hell-hole in the nick of time. All right, where does this Pool kid live? I'm gonna have myself a little talk with him."

"Right around the block, just off Maple. Big grey job. You can't miss it."

Victor put the key into the ignition. "Don't breathe a word of this to anyone, Gus. I mean it."

Gus stepped out of the car. "Hell no," he said. "Tell you what, though. When the search parties come around the diner, I'll let them know the woods ain't the focus anymore. I'll say…

the case is under control now, and the trooper will get the word out if he needs any more help. How's that?"

———

"*You're the cream in my coffee, you're the salt in my stew.*" Jack sat on the edge of his bunk, singing the popular song and accompanying himself on the cello. "*You will always be my ne-cess-i-ty, I'd be lost without you.*"

He'd just spent a dreamy hour practicing his audition piece, a Vivaldi concerto, all the time imagining himself playing first chair with the New York Philharmonic, sounding just like the records he listened to on the Victrola—rich, deep, like liquid chocolate.

"*All alone, I'm so all alone,*" he crooned. "*There is no one else but you. All alone by the telephone waiting for a ring, a ting-a-ling.*" At the Bentley School, he'd be able to study and perform both classical and pop music, and that, he figured, would up his chances of turning a dream into a career. Performer, composer, teacher—or maybe all three—he didn't know. All he knew was that music was as natural and necessary to him as breathing.

Jack put away his cello and picked up his *shofar.* Rabbi Abrams had chosen him to blow the ram's horn, the most ancient of Jewish musical instruments, this year at Yom Kippur services, and he wanted to sound good. This would be, after all, a performance of sorts. The ridges of the curved horn fit well in his hands as he forced air into the rim to produce the powerful blasts. He sounded several short notes and then the longest one he could hold.

Yom Kippur services were long. Some people would come and go, especially the ones with small children, but Jack would stay. The only time he'd leave the building would be for *Yizkor*, the special prayer of remembrance for people who'd lost a loved one. Those lucky enough to have intact families waited outside the temple doors. Both of Jack's parents stayed inside. So did Jack's friend Abe Goldberg. Meanwhile, everyone waiting outside knew that one day they'd move inside to recite the *Yizkor* prayer, and that sometime later, the prayer would be said for them.

When Jack released the last note, he sat up and stared out his window. He could see the Main Street Bridge standing vigil over the St. Lawrence, which, in another few miles, would enter Canada on its journey east to the Atlantic. He thought about his father's voyage along this waterway on his way to America. Mr. Pool said it was the coldest weather he'd ever known—January in Quebec—and that the ferrymen showed him how to test the temperature. "Go outside and spit," they'd said. "If it freezes the second it hits the ground, then it's twenty below. But if it freezes in midair, then it's at least forty below. Either way, the ferries don't run."

If only Mr. Pool had entered America through Ellis Island like thousands of others, his family would probably be living in Brooklyn or Boston or some other city. Then Jack would have music schools at his fingertips, and concerts and sheet music shops. But Mr. Pool's poor vision prevented all that. When he immigrated, people were so afraid of trachoma—a contagious, blinding disease—that if your eyes didn't seem quite right, you could be standing right next to the Statue of Liberty and still get sent back to your homeland. So he didn't risk it. He came in through Canada instead, first to Montreal, then across the St. Lawrence to Northern New York State.

Jack cursed his father's eyes.

And yet, if he had been able to see, Mr. Pool might not have come to America at all. He might have stayed in his *shtetl*—Zininka, one of the many Russian ghettos where the Jews were forced to live but were forbidden from owning land, attending school, or practicing the more profitable trades. He might have endured the empty belly, the isolation, the encroaching violence against the Jews. But word had it that American doctors could restore eyesight. Jack's father could live without food or security, but he desperately, urgently wanted to see. And so he came.

Of course he came. Who wouldn't, if it meant being able to see clearly for the first time? Jack thought the only thing worse than blindness would be deafness, because then there'd be no music. Having no music would be like having no language, no passion, no inspiration. He couldn't bear the thought.

When Mr. Pool found out that the American cure didn't exist, there was only one thing left to do: he threw on a shoulder pack and walked from town to town, peddling notions and a little clothing. "Lucky for me I can weigh the difference between a five-spot and a ten in my hands," he'd joke. After a couple of years he bought a horse and wagon so he could travel farther, and that's how he met his future wife in Santa Clara.

When Jack's parents opened Pool's Dry Goods, Massena was enjoying the tail end of an odd sort of heyday—thanks to its stinking water, of all things. The Mohawks had discovered a sulfur-water spring at the edge of town just after the War Between the States, and people believed it could cure a slew of conditions. Visitors started coming from all over the country, as well as from Canada and Europe. Even the Netherlands' Queen Wilhelmina, who supposedly had a bad case of eczema, made a point of stopping by during one of her U.S. visits.

By the turn of the century, fancy guesthouses circled the springs. Entire families checked in with their servants for a week or two at a time, bathing in the rank water and glopping on the rotten mud. Soon, laborers moved in to work as cooks, housekeepers and maids. Local boys made extra money on weekends as dippers, lugging large canisters of sulfur water to the bathtubs of guests who were too rich or too lazy to go outside.

Then the craze passed. The laborers left town, and the guesthouses stood mostly empty. Massena was no longer special, no longer noticed. Colorless, featureless, bland. Just another pit town on the river.

The Bentley School will be my ticket out of here, Jack told himself, gripping the *shofar.* First to Syracuse for two years, then maybe to a conservatory in New York City or Boston. After that, anything would be possible.

"*Birds do it, bees do it, even lazy jellyfish do it. Let's do it…let's fall in love,*" he sang absently. "*I'm sure sometimes on the sly you do it. Maybe even you and I might do it. Let's do it, let's fall in love.*"

Jack took up his cello again, but the doorbell rang before he could begin. He thought it might be Abe Goldberg, or maybe Mrs. Kauffman delivering her famous cheese blintzes, or even his own father, who sometimes forgot his house key. But when he heard his mother saying, "Yes?" in the same wary tone she used with traveling salesmen, he knew it must be a stranger. *But at 8:15 in the evening? That's odd.* Setting his cello aside, he went downstairs to see who it was.

"Can I help you?" Mrs. Pool was asking. She was talking to a cop—a tall man with a red mustache, a dark uniform shining with brass buttons, and a sheath of stubble starting to shadow his cheeks.

Jack's chest clamped. What was a cop doing at his house? Where was his father?

"Evening," the officer said. "Trooper Victor Brown here. I'm calling for some help with the missing girl."

"Missing girl?" Jack and his mother asked in unison, stepping out of the doorway to let him in.

"It's been on the radio—and the street—all day."

"I don't play the radio on the Sabbath," Mrs. Pool said.

"It ain't Sunday yet, ma'am," Victor said.

"Yes, but our—" She pressed her lips shut. "What girl?"

"Daisy Durham. Mrs. Jenna Durham's daughter."

"Daisy?" Jack said.

"What? How long has she been gone?" Mrs. Pool asked.

"Since around one," the trooper said. "A long time. Half the town is out looking for her. Her mother's been trying to get you all afternoon."

"I don't answer the phone on the Sabbath, either," she said. "Daisy did spend the morning with us. My son walked her home—she went straight home. Oh, this is terrible. How can I help?"

"Actually, ma'am, the reason I'm here is, I'd like to talk to your son. Is this him here?"

"Yes," Jack said.

"Your name is Jack?"

"Yes."

"I'd like to ask you a few things, if you don't mind."

"Why?" Mrs. Pool asked.

"Just fact-checking, ma'am, that's all. Sort of retracing Daisy's steps."

"I guess that would be all right. Come in." She led him to the kitchen table and then stood by the stove, pretending to watch over the already-cooked soup. The trooper glanced around the kitchen, sniffed a few times quickly, grimaced, and swallowed—all so quick, you wouldn't have noticed unless you were watching. Which Jack was.

He took a seat. The trooper straddled the chair opposite him. "So then, you weren't aware that Daisy's gone missing?" he asked.

"No. I walked her home right at noon and haven't heard anything since. I worked all afternoon and part of the evening, then I came back here."

"That so? I'm told you were down at the diner this evening."

"Oh, yeah. I was. I stopped at the Sit Down for a bite on my way home from work." He paused. "I didn't know that was important."

"I'm told you were talking about Daisy there. So I'm just wondering—"

Mrs. Pool slammed the lid on the soup pot and started toward the table, but Jack motioned for her to wait. "I didn't talk to anybody about Daisy," he said. "Why would I, when I didn't even know she was missing?"

The trooper didn't say anything.

"I don't know where Daisy is, Officer," Jack went on. "If I did, I'd tell you."

"I believe you, Jack. Of *course* you don't know where Daisy is. But let me ask you this. Do you have any guesses—just guesses—about how she might have disappeared?"

"Now listen here," Mrs. Pool said. "You have no right—"

"Okay, listen, both of you," the trooper said. "Jack. Mrs. Pool. I'm gonna give it to you plain. I'm told you people believe a sacrifice—a blood sacrifice of a Christian child—is proper in celebrating your holidays. You have a holiday coming up, right? And now we have a Christian child missing out of the blue. So it's only logical for me to suppose..."

Jack and his mother stared at the trooper. Blood sacrifice? *Blood sacrifice?*

Jack wished his mother would start to cry. Someone needed to cry, and he didn't want to be the one. Then for an instant, he thought he might laugh. He thought his churning belly and his burning throat might erupt in a full-out spasm of laughter. But that instant passed quickly, giving way to gagging fear.

"*Oh my God!*" he heard his mother roar. "Get out of my house! Take your horrid lies and get out of here!"

"Ma'am, easy." Victor stood up. "I'm just checking out possibilities."

"*Out!*" she shouted, grabbing her broomstick from the corner and pointing the handle at him. "Get out of my house!"

By this time, Harry and Martha had abandoned their spy post in the next room and were gaping in the kitchen doorway. "Mama?" Martha asked, wide-eyed.

"I said get out." Mrs. Pool's voice turned quiet and low, like a growl, and she raised the broom a little higher. "But tell me one thing first. What does Jenna Durham have to say about this stupid idea of yours?"

"She doesn't know. Not from me, anyway. She took to bed some time ago."

"Good. Now go." She took a step closer and shoved the broomstick under his nose.

"This isn't over," Victor said, taking a step back. "Not nearly." He turned around and strode quickly out of the house. Jack heard the click of the door lock and the thump of the broom returning to the corner, and then his mother was sitting next to him at the table, her hands clenched and her cheeks crimson.

———

"Back upstairs, both of you," Mrs. Pool ordered Harry and Martha. "You can take down my Chinese checkers set if you wish, but don't come down until I call you. Hurry now."

Mrs. Pool asked Jack, "Are you all right?"

Jack folded his arms on the kitchen table and let out an unsteady breath. "I guess."

"Jack, what happened at the diner?"

"Nothing. I sat at the counter, and Gus asked me why I was working so late. I told him we were trying to get a shipment unpacked before the holy day. That's all. Then I ate my eggs and left."

"Are you certain that's all?"

"Don't you believe me?"

"Of course I do. I'm just trying to figure out who the liar is — the real Jew-hating liar. Who else was there?"

"I don't know, there were a bunch. Roy Royman. Old Man Claghorn. Bucky Sanborn. A bunch. Mama, what did I do?"

"You didn't do anything. And don't you worry — we won't be seeing any more of that trooper, not if he knows what's good for him. But that poor child. And Jenna. The worst thing that could happen to a mother."

"I need to go help look for Daisy." He started to stand up.

She put her hand on his shoulder. "Absolutely not! They'd sooner see you hanged than let you help."

"But—"

"But nothing. You stay put. Don't you have some potatoes to peel?"

"Potatoes?"

"A basket of them. In the sink."

"But shouldn't we—"

"No. Go on now. Do as I say." She got up and went straight to the telephone in the hallway, where she asked the operator to put her through to Jenna Durham. "Hello, Durham residence?" she said. "Eva Pool calling. Who is this? ...Oh, Clarisse. I just heard. I'm so very sorry. Is Jenna available?...I see. Poor dear. Well, I don't want to disturb her if she's resting, of course. I'll try her again later...I shouldn't?...Yes, I understand. I'll wait to hear from you, then. You will let me know if there's anything, anything at all, I can do, won't you?... Yes, of course. Good night, Clarisse."

Next, Mrs. Pool asked the operator for Pool's Dry Goods. As Jack listened to her whisper into the receiver, he knew the truth. If his mother couldn't wait to talk until Mr. Pool got home, then she was plenty worried.

———

"Let's head back," Lydie said when they reached the river. "Daisy's not around here anywhere."

Emaline hesitated. She listened to the water break on the rocky bank and wondered how fast the current could carry a little girl's body. Maybe Daisy's bloated corpse would get so far downriver before washing up that the people who found her wouldn't know about her. Maybe they'd bury her in an unmarked grave, and she'd never be laid to rest next to her own father.

The Sacred Heart bells rang nine. "Why isn't anyone out here helping?" Emaline asked impatiently.

"I don't know, but we should really head back."

"If you think so," Emaline said, but she didn't move. "Do you want to hear something awful?"

"No."

"This morning I told Daisy she was a great big pest. She got into my beads, the ones I'm using for Ma's birthday bracelet, and I was so cross, I said, 'Daisy Elizabeth Durham, if I were rich, the first thing I'd do is get my own house.' I think that might've been the last thing I ever said to her."

"Hush now." Lydie pulled her close. "It might've been the last thing you said to her this morning, but you'll have plenty of chances to make up with her."

"How do you know?" Emaline squeezed her eyes shut, but the tears escaped anyway, rolling down her cheeks to her lips, where she licked them away.

Lydie reached into her coat pocket and brought out a handkerchief. "You know, you're just punishing yourself. And I'll bet your mother is sitting at home doing the same thing, going over everything she said today, everything she didn't say. Where's that getting her? I ask you. More important, where's it getting Daisy? We've got to keep ourselves pulled together now, for Daisy's sake."

"I don't think I can anymore. I'm all balled up, and my legs are so tired, they feel like applesauce."

"Come on, then. Let's get you home. A hot bath and a hot drink will do you good."

"Okay, but I'm going barefoot. My heels are screaming with blisters."

"Good idea." Lydie stepped out of her shoes and picked up one in each hand. "The ground's nice and cool. All right, let's go."

"Look," Emaline said as they walked. "Even fewer flashlights than before. They're giving up. Just like us."

"We're not giving up. We're just giving up on this one course. Besides, look at us. We can hardly walk."

"I don't think I've walked this much all year," Emaline confessed. "But if we've traveled so far, then why can't we find her?" There, she said it. The dreaded question.

"We'll figure that out when we get to your house. Come on, our flashlight's fading."

"Ahhh!" Emaline cried, stopping short.

Lydie started, coughing uncontrollably. "What is it?" she wheezed.

"Must've stepped on a stick or something. I'll be all right. What's wrong with you?"

Lydie made a few more barking coughs, then swallowed hard. "When you cried out, I swallowed my gum. Never mind." Lydie shined the dying flashlight on Emaline's foot, exposing a few drops of blood. "It's not too bad, but it needs a good cleaning. Here, lean on my shoulder and we'll take it slower." Emaline put her arm around her cousin, and they crept on.

———

"What's gonna happen to Daisy?" Martha knelt on a kitchen chair next to Jack while he peeled a crateful of red potatoes over the sink. Harry was shucking corn on the porch, and Mr. and Mrs. Pool were retrieving linens upstairs. They were speaking to each other in Yiddish, so whatever they were saying, they didn't want their children to know.

Martha brushed her dark hair out of her face. "What's gonna happen to her?"

"They're gonna find her, that's what," Jack said. He used the tip of the paring knife to dig out a particularly deep eye. "Pretty soon you'll be doing this work too, squirt," he said, handing her another potato for the pot.

"How do you know?"

"Because we all do this work."

"No, I mean, how do you know they're gonna find her?"

"Because. Because she didn't disappear into thin air. She got lost, and someone will find her, that's all." He sensed her staring up at him, so he fastened his eyes on hers. "I said, someone will find her."

"How 'bout you?"

"How 'bout me what?"

"How 'bout you find her, silly," she said, climbing up on the counter and dangling her legs over the edge.

He let out a small laugh. *If only I could go out and look for Daisy*, he thought. *If only I wasn't accused of killing her.*

"Well, why dontcha?"

"Can't, silly. I've got to peel these potatoes." *Martha's right—I should be out with the search parties. After all, if Daisy vanished right after I left her in her driveway, isn't it my fault? Why didn't I wait for her to get inside her house? Or maybe I did wait. Did I watch her push open the door—or not?* It was no use. He couldn't remember. At this point, he couldn't distinguish between reality and wishful thinking.

"Agh," he muttered when the knife slipped from the potato and cut a shallow crevice in his finger. He squeezed the finger with the opposite hand and watched the trickle of blood leak out. A cut on his fingering hand. Why did it have to be his fingering hand? Mr. Morse always told Jack to treat his fingers like the precious things they were. Now look what he'd done—with his audition only three days away. *Nothing can interfere with that, nothing. I've got to get to Syracuse. And I've got to get out of here.*

"What's the matter, Jackie?" Martha asked.

"Nothing. Listen, squirt, someone will find her. I promise, all right? Now let me finish my work."

A promise from her big brother seemed to be enough to satisfy Martha. She handed Jack a fat potato and hopped off the counter to find Mrs. Pool, leaving him with a sink full of browning vegetable skins. Dropping the knife into the sink, he watched a thick splash of blood disappear down the drain.

There was no denying one thing: regardless of when or how Daisy disappeared, he had been blamed. Accused. As good as convicted.

Why?

And, more importantly, where—where would this monstrous lie about Jews using blood in their rituals lead? How many people would hear it, believe it, act on it? Does Emaline know I'm suspected of murdering her sister?

Rabbi Abrams said rumors were about as easy to unspread as butter. Was it too late already? Were the Jew-haters coalescing even now? Would word of this circulate as far as Syracuse, as far as Dean Elihu Pierson's office? Would all his plans and years of hard work get wiped out just like that, all because of a lie? *God*, Jack thought as he pressed a dishtowel to his cut hand, *let it be over. And let my promise to Martha not be broken. Amen.*

———

Clarisse waited for the girls to get back before heading home. "Don't disturb your mother," she told Emaline on her way out. "She said she wants to get some rest. Lydie, you coming with me?"

"No, I'm going to stay with Em."

"Okay, well, it's 9:30 now. I'll call at 11 to check in."

"No, Mother. You get yourself some rest. We'll call you if there's news."

"Well..."

"Good night, Aunt Clarisse," Emaline said.

As soon as Clarisse bustled out of the house, Lydie said, "C'mon, Em, let's go see your ma. If she told Mother she needs a rest that means she needs a rest from Mother, that's all."

They headed upstairs and stopped outside Mrs. Durham's door. "I'm home," Emaline said. *God, if I could only hear Daisy say those words.*

"Come in," she said. "It's not locked."

Emaline winced when she saw her mother sitting up in bed, looking so pasty and frail. Even her hair seemed to have lost its color. *Like the life has been siphoned right out of her.*

"Thank heavens, it's you two," Mrs. Durham said. "Those women kept pestering me to eat a sandwich or drink some tea, so I finally just told them I had to lie down."

"Well, Mother was the last of them," Lydie said, "and now she's gone too, thank goodness."

Emaline raised an eyebrow.

"I'm just being honest," Lydie said. "We all know she's bossy and she talks too much. Not to mention that she's a worrywart."

"She's had hard times too," Mrs. Durham said. "You can't blame her for being twitchy. Come here, sit with me, both of you. And bring me my rosary, would you? On the bureau."

Emaline handed her the rosary and sat at the foot of the bed next to Lydie. Mrs. Durham stroked the beads and then let them fall onto the quilt. "Do you know what a wretched soul I am?" she asked. "I told Daisy she couldn't have her lunch today till she came back from hollering for you. She's been gone all these hours, and she doesn't even have a decent meal in her. Not even a biscuit. And wearing last year's spring coat. Barely covers her knees anymore."

Emaline glanced at Lydie and scooted closer to her mother. "Stop that, Ma. We knew you'd be doing this, being hard on yourself for things that aren't your fault. Why don't we talk about something different? Then we can go back to fretting."

Mrs. Durham turned her face to the window as if she expected to see Daisy bouncing up the front walk in her too-short spring coat.

"Ma, did you hear me?"

"How about you read to me? There's a book under the water pitcher. Read me something from it. Something sad."

"Something sad? That's no good. How about something—"

"No, I want something sad."

Emaline pulled out the book and started thumbing through it.

"Your father gave me that book when you were born,"

Mrs. Durham said. "I used to read it when I was up with you at night."

"Was I up much?"

"All the time, but I didn't mind."

"You didn't mind being up all night?"

"Your father stayed up with me. We took turns holding you, and I'd read out loud when it wasn't my turn. If you hadn't kept us up, I'd have missed that time with him. Now read me something."

Emaline continued scanning the pages. "Okay, how about this:

Sorrow like a ceaseless rain
 Beats upon my heart.
People twist and scream in pain—
Dawn will find them still again;
This has neither wax nor wane,
 Neither stop nor start.
People dress and go to town;
 I sit in my chair.
All my thoughts are slow and brown:
Standing up or sitting down
Little matters, or what gown
 Or what shoes I wear."

"Brown," Mrs. Durham said. "That's the right color. Not black, not red, not grey. Brown. You spend years thinking the worst possible tragedy has already befallen you, and then something even more dreadful happens, and all you can do is sit there." She closed her eyes.

"Why don't you try to sleep now, Ma?"

"Sleep? I can't sleep. But you should rest. You must be exhausted. You too, Lydie."

They couldn't deny it. They were bone-tired.

"Go," she urged. "I need you to be rested."

Emaline nodded, although she wasn't sure she'd ever be able to sleep again. "You'll wake us if...?"

"Of course. Now go. Find Lydie a pillow. And pull out an extra quilt if you need it."

———

Victor and Gus took the table nearest the window fan, coffee cups in hand.

"Find anything out?" Gus asked.

"Only that the Pool kid and his mother are full of excuses. Contradicting themselves left and right about where they were tonight and why they didn't answer the phone this afternoon. And a big icy mitt from the lady at the end. I'm thinking it's time to check their store."

"I made you a list of all the Jew businesses in town." Gus pushed a folded piece of paper across the table. "Just in case the Pool place don't check out."

Victor cracked open the paper. "One, two, three...eight. Jeezus, that's gotta be half the stores in town."

"You should know. Your father knew. The Jews move in and take over every money-making operation in sight."

"This could take hours."

"It's not that big a town. These places are all on the same couple of blocks." Gus plunked down his coffee cup and leaned forward. "Do it for your father, Victor. Do it for the man who had to drive a cab to put food on your table."

"Bus."

"Huh?"

"It was a bus. Anyways, I'll start with the Pool joint and go from there."

"Wait, let me jot down their preacher's address—Abrams. He has all the right tools for this kinda job—I shoulda thought of that before."

"Tools?"

"He keeps an old piano box in his backyard. I seen them Jews bringing him live chickens—they all raise their own chickens—and he takes the birds out back to his box and comes back with them dead. Sometimes they even bring him a live cow. They walk the animal right down to his house on a rope like they own the street and they have him slaughter it. Then someone comes to pick up the cow parts with a truck."

"No kidding?"

"It's unreal. Anyway, if you like, I can come up with a list of their home addresses too. Just in case. Just so you know you're hitting on all sixes."

"Later, Gus. I'm hoping I won't need to go that far."

"Attaboy."

———

Harry and Jack were sitting on the front steps shucking the last of the corn into a paper bag when the police car pulled up to the house.

"What now?" asked Harry.

"Come on," Jack said, brushing corn silk from his trousers and moving quickly down the steps. He didn't want the trooper to get to the front door. His parents were inside, putting Martha to bed.

"Is your father at home?" Victor asked as he approached the boys in the driveway.

"No," Jack lied. "Can I help you with something?"

"It's about his establishment. I need to check it."

Jack nudged himself in front of Harry. "Establishment? The store? Check the store?"

"Yeah, have a look around. The Durham girl is nowhere to be found. So we're going to search the places of business."

"You're going to check *all* the businesses in town? Even the farms?"

"Not all."

"Just the Jewish businesses. That's what you mean, isn't it?"

Victor wouldn't look at him. He stroked his mustache and watched the moths orbiting the lantern on the porch.

"It's ten at night," Jack said. "You need to get into the store now?"

"The sooner the better."

"Well, our father's not home. I'll let you in. Hold on, let me get the key." Pulling Harry along with him, Jack went inside and grabbed the spare store key that hung from a pantry hook. "Don't say anything to Mama or Pa until they figure out I'm gone."

"Are you kidding? They'll have our heads for this."

"Don't worry, I'll take all the blame. Close the door behind me, would you?"

Jack ran out of the house. "You have no right to do this," he told Victor as they headed for the car.

"I'm afraid I do, kid," Victor said, opening the back door. "I have every right when a child's life is at stake. Now get in."

Jack fell into the seat. He'd never been in a police car and thought he never would. It smelled like cigarettes and rubber.

As Victor pulled away from the curb and drove down the street, Jack's head filled with nightmarish images. He saw his baseball team huddled up the way they did right before a game started. Of course, Jack wasn't in the huddle, because he was never at the Saturday games. But Moose Doyle was there. Trooper Brown was there too. So was automobile king Henry Ford, who'd recently published *The International Jew: The World's Foremost Problem*, and he was handing out free copies of his book. Joining the group was a pack of men Jack didn't recognize at first. Then he realized it was the gang that had lynched Leo Frank in Atlanta.

Poor Leo Frank. He was the manager of the National Pencil Factory in 1913 when a thirteen-year-old girl who worked there was found strangled. Leo Frank was accused of murder and convicted on circumstantial evidence. But before he could begin serving his life-imprisonment sentence, he was kidnapped and hanged by a group that included a former governor, the son of a U.S. Senator, bankers, doctors and a sheriff. None of the lynchers were prosecuted. Half the Jews in Georgia fled the state.

Jack tried to move to a different part of his mind. The opening chords of the concerto in C minor. The solid feeling of the cello between his knees. The warmth of the carved maple neck against his thumb. But it was no use.

Victor pulled in front of Pool's Dry Goods, where ten or maybe fifteen men were standing on the curb, drinking coffee and smoking cigarettes, as if they'd been waiting for them. They raised their cups in salute and moved aside to let the trooper park.

Jack suddenly felt compelled to study the faces in the

crowd—to watch and memorize them—but he fought the urge. He didn't want them to see the fear in his eyes, and he didn't want to see the hate in theirs. Instead, he gazed upward, where he saw a smashed egg drizzling down the store sign. He wondered if Gus Poulos had provided the egg from the diner.

Then Victor was opening his door and motioning him out of the car, telling the crowd to make way. Jack took the key from his pocket, and, with imaginary blinders on, unlocked the store and disappeared inside, Victor at his heels.

Jack hit the light switch, and Victor started walking the perimeter of the store. He probed the racks of trousers and felt behind the cabinets. He stood on tiptoes to check the wall shelves. Then he poked his head into the fitting room and the tiny bathroom in the back.

Jack stepped away from the door so the crowd outside couldn't see him. *My God*, he thought, watching Victor open cupboards and drawers. *He actually expects to find little body parts scattered around. He thinks he's going to uncover fingers and kneecaps, teeth and organs, if he just looks hard enough.*

"Holy Jesus!" said Victor from the shoe closet.

"Sir?"

"Aw, hell," Victor grumbled, "it's just a mannequin on its side. There a basement here?"

Jack pointed to the staircase between the men's jackets and the women's flannels. Victor headed down and started turning over shipping crates, shoving aside spare tables, and rifling through merchandise. *He's wrecking the place*, Jack realized, *and he's going to leave the mess for me to pick up.*

Then an even worse thought gripped him: the Sabbath wine! Mr. Pool hid the wine bottles in the basement joists—

in the fourth row from the left, to be precise, so he could
always find with his hands what he couldn't with his eyes.
If the trooper found the illegal alcohol, what would he do?
Fortunately, Victor never looked up.

———

"All right," said Victor, rounding the top of the stairs, "let's get
you home. I've got a long night ahead. Go on to the car."

Jack didn't go on though. He was waiting for the trooper
to finish his thought—to apologize, or at least to thank Jack
for his cooperation. It didn't happen. Finally, Jack did as he
was told.

The crowd rushed closer when the store door reopened.
"Didja find her?" one shadow asked. Another called out,
"Fools, go back in there!" And then they all started jabbering
at once. Jack quickly locked the store door and ducked
into the car, turning his back on all of them. If any of his
baseball team was there, he didn't want to know. If any of
his neighbors, teachers, or so-called friends were out there,
he didn't want to know that, either. Better to let them be a
faceless swarm of bugs.

Victor, still standing on the sidewalk, cleared his throat.
"Gentlemen. Gentlemen, please. We're making progress, and
now I advise you all to go home. We'll keep you apprised. In
the meantime, please clear the sidewalk and the road."

The gang grumbled, nodded, swore, spat and kicked the
curb as Victor got into the car. He pulled out and made a
U-turn that sent half the auto up on the opposite sidewalk. An
egg arched through the air before smashing on a rear tire.

One of Jack's cello solos started playing in his head,

one that began *agitato*—played in an agitated mood—and progressed to *furioso*—furious. Yes, that was exactly how he felt, *agitato* and *furioso*. Then his mind gave way to a different score, one that was *pesante*—heavy—and *mèsto*—mournful. Knotting his fingers together, he could feel the torn skin where the potato knife had sliced him, and he wondered how long it would take to heal. *As long as it's all right in time for Syracuse. As long as I can still play my music.*

The trip home felt much shorter than the trip to the store. It seemed like the egg was still smacking against the tire when the car jerked to a stop at the foot of the Pool's driveway. Jack's parents were planted like solemn statues on the front stoop. It was going to be a long night for everyone, and they all knew it.

———

Emaline bolted upright in bed.

"Em, what is it?" asked Lydie, who was lying next to her in the bed.

"I had a crazy, awful dream, it was about Daisy, she was in a boat on the river—no, not exactly, more like a raft on a pond, she was calling to me, she was saying...*God, I can't remember what it was.*"

Emaline swung her feet onto the floor and covered her face with her hands. "It felt so real, what if it means something, what if it's a clue?—if I could just bring it back." It was no use, though. The dream had vanished.

"I don't believe in that stuff," Lydie said firmly, putting her hand on Emaline's back. "Dreams are dreams, and real life is real life, and that's all."

"I guess so. Sorry I woke you."

"No need. Listen, I hear your mother in the kitchen. How about we go keep her company?"

———

Jack watched his mother step cautiously to the phone stand in the hallway. After resting her hand on the receiver for several seconds, she picked it up and asked the operator to connect her to the rabbi's house. There was no answer. Next, she asked for Sophie Popkin, but immediately remembered that the Popkins were out of town for the holy days. "Put me through to Anna Friedman instead, would you?" she said.

"Hello, Anna, this is Eva Pool. Forgive me for calling so late—I know it's after eleven...I am well, thank you. I just wanted to let you know that you might be getting a visitor tonight...No, not that. It's in connection with the little girl who's gone missing...Yes, it's terrible, isn't it? Do you know the family?...Anyway, there's a search going on, and the police are making some stops, so don't be surprised if you hear from them...You're most welcome. Perhaps I'll call again later tonight or in the morning then? Good-bye, dear."

"Mama, that's never going to work," Jack said. "You need to be more direct if you want anyone to understand that their store is about to get raided."

"I don't trust those party lines one bit. There are too many gossips with nothing better to do than eavesdrop on other people's conversations. I don't want to accidentally spread this rumor any further than it's already gotten."

"But—"

"You let me handle this my own way," she said and was about to pick up the receiver again when the phone rang.

"Hello?...Oh, Dr. Levine, is everything all right? Be careful how you say it, now...You too? I knew the other storekeepers were in for it, but your medical office?...Yes, I know. Did he say where he was going next or...I see...Well, I was just about to call the Kauffmans and Kaplans. If you want to try reaching Dr. Grunbaum and, let's see, maybe the Liptons, that would help...Yes, yes, I'll stay in touch. You too."

"Jack," she said when she hung up, "I want you to take Harry and Martha into my bedroom and lock yourselves in there. Carry Martha in and tell her everything's all right."

"But Mama—"

"No buts. I have calls to make, and that's where I want the three of you."

"For how long?"

"Until I say so."

"But I can help you."

The phone rang again. Mrs. Pool gave Jack her I-mean-it look. He left to find Martha and Harry.

———

At 11:30, Martha was curled up under an Adirondack blanket, asleep on her parents' bed, and Harry was stretched out on the floor, trying to lose himself in the latest issue of *Life* magazine. Jack sat in the rocking chair near the window, holding his *shofar* and studying a crack that zigzagged its way across the ceiling. He was thinking, thinking and wondering, and suddenly he was agonizing: *What will they do to me if Daisy is found hurt? Or dead? Or if she's never found—what then?* An image of a bleak stinking prison cell seized his thoughts. And right behind that the body of Leo Frank—strung from a tree branch, his neck snapping against the rope, a crowd below him kicking and spitting on his dangling body.

Outside somewhere, he could hear muffled voices, but all he could see through the window were a few lit houses and, thanks to its slightly elevated position at the top of Hill Street, the south side of the synagogue. He tried harder to focus on the ceiling fissure. When Martha rolled dreamily from her back to her side, he murmured, "Must be nice."

"What must be nice?" Harry asked.

"To be able to sleep."

Downstairs, the phone sounded, as it had been doing every few minutes, and someone picked up on the first ring. "Harry, open the door," Jack said. "Just a little. I want to hear."

Harry got up and cracked the door, letting in dribs and drabs of Mrs. Pool's voice. "Now, Hannah," she was saying. "All Albert will have to do is let him in and...Yes, go inside the shop with him...Just him, just the one, I expect...Call me..."

Outside, the voices abruptly turned into sharp bellows. Harry jumped back and Jack jumped up, the cold heat of panic sweeping up his insides and spilling down his skin. *Are they coming to get me—to drag me to the lockup or the noose? What do they want me to do, or do they want to do something to me?* Down to his very core, Jack was afraid, and he hated everyone responsible for his fear—the trooper, the crowds, the whole town. He even hated himself.

"We should go to the cellar," Harry said. He had his nightshirt on but hadn't taken off his trousers yet, and he absent-mindedly tried to tuck the nightshirt into his pants. "C'mon."

Jack didn't answer.

"Come on," Harry repeated.

"Shhh, you'll wake Martha up," Jack whispered. "Listen, we're not going anywhere. The basement's no safer than here. It's worse—the lock on that damned Bilco door is practically rusted out. Just hold your horses."

Harry untucked his half-tucked nightshirt, sat on the floor cross-legged, and sighed melodramatically. "Hey, doesn't that sound like Scottie Logan's father out there? He never liked us, you know."

"What makes you think that?" Jack asked, moving closer to the window. He thought he heard a girl's voice, but the street was black, and he couldn't see anyone.

"Because. Because once I heard Mr. Logan tell Scottie that God made Jews ugly for the same reason He put rattles on snakes: to warn their prey."

"What? You never told me about that."

"Why should I? I bet you don't tell me every dumb thing you hear."

"Yeah, well, who else do you hear out there?"

Harry paused to listen. "Can't tell. They aren't so close anymore."

It was true. The shouts were moving down the street, and then they turned the corner and disappeared. The hush echoed in Jack's ears. For a moment, one glimmering moment, he allowed himself to believe that the crowd had nothing to do with Daisy or him. Maybe it was just a bunch of partygoers, on their way home from an evening of dancing and laughing and eating finger cakes.

But no. Those were Jew-haters out there. Of that, he hadn't a shred of doubt.

"What do we do now?" asked Harry.

"Let's forget about all that. They're probably just some jerks full of giggle water, that's all."

"You mean...?"

"I bet they're fried to the hat. Hey, look, how about you and me play a game? Twenty questions or something."

"A game? Why?"

"No reason, just a change of pace. Maybe we could—" A strange sound downstairs cut him off.

"Wh-what's that?" Harry breathed.

Jack was already at the door. "I'm going down."

"I'll go with you," said Harry, springing up.

"No. You can't."

"But—"

"But nothing. You stay here with Martha."

Harry lowered his head and sank back onto the floor.

"Look," Jack said. "It's your job to take care of Martha, all right? We can't both go down there, and we both shouldn't be up here. Lock the door behind me."

When Jack got to the living room, he found his father clutching a rock the size of a baseball and his mother picking up glass shards from the rug and dropping them into her apron pocket—the same pocket where she kept her story pad and pencil. Jack wondered what story she might write about this later tonight, when she couldn't sleep. Would she tell the truth, or would she write herself into the saner world of her imagination?

"Mama?" Jack said.

Mrs. Pool straightened up. "Jack, get back in the bedroom, and keep everyone away from the window."

"But I can do this for you."

"No. I want you upstairs. With the door locked."

The fear on her face alarmed him. Part of him wanted to run back upstairs to his hiding place. Besides, he already had one sliced finger; what if the glass made more cuts? What if he couldn't play his Vivaldi piece properly? But his mother shouldn't have to do this alone. And yet...

Jack stood there, the cool air sweeping over his face, when the phone rang. Mrs. Pool went to the hallway to answer it. "Hello?...Yes, Benny, I'm listening..."

"This is a good rock," Mr. Pool said to Jack. "Not like what you trip on in the street. More the kind you go looking for. Round, like fist. Good for throwing. Like throwing a fist." He looked old and brittle in the yellow lamplight, like a worn cornhusk that might dissolve into a pile of dust at any second.

"What about the rabbi?" Jack asked. "Has anyone told him?"

The outside voices became audible again, although only as a distant whir. "I call the rabbi's house a hundred times," Mr. Pool said. "Must be he is at *shul*."

"Do you want me to go get him? I could—"

"No! You are not to leave the house again."

"But—"

"Jack," Mr. Pool said, setting down the rock on the lamp stand. "What can the rabbi do tonight? Let him finish making ready for Yom Kippur. In the daylight, we talk to him."

"He used his gun to get in?" Mrs. Pool was saying from the other room. "But—now watch what you say over the phone, Benny...And then what? He just left?"

"Son of a bitch!" Jack kicked the baseboard.

"Easy," said his father. "A broken window, that is bad enough. We don't need any broken walls."

"Yes," said Mrs. Pool, "it would be good of you to do that... Good night, Benny." She replaced the receiver and walked briskly back into the living room, looking ashen.

"What was that about?" Mr. Pool asked.

"Simon Slavin's dress shop. Si's in Albany for the holy days, and when he wasn't there to let the trooper in, the trooper let himself in. Used the butt of his gun to smash the shop window and climbed right in. Went through the place—must have taken him all of one minute, it's so tiny—and then just left the store wide open." She picked up another piece of glass and rolled it over in her hands. "And what are you still doing down here, Jack? Martha and Harry are up there alone."

"Jack, get yourself some rest," Mr. Pool added. "It will be all right."

"All right?" Jack half-laughed. "How can things be all right? Nothing will ever be all right." He turned toward the stairs in anticipation of a cold, sleepless night.

———

"Thank God that's over," Gus said. He piled the last case of whiskey into the cab of the truck which Roy Royman had parked twenty yards from the river at the edge of Paradise Woods.

The two men climbed in and slammed their doors shut. "It's not one in the morning yet," Royman said. "That wasn't as bad as I expected."

"Thanks to me." Gus bit off the end of a fresh cigar and held it between his teeth, unlit. "Dimwit trooper!"

"Well, we both know you're the brains behind the operation. I'm just the muscles and good looks."

"Never mind that. Just let's move this load to the shed so we can be done with it. I'm telling you, if this stuff wasn't liquid gold, it wouldn't be worth half the trouble."

As Royman started the engine, Gus looked out into the blackness of the woods, wondering if Daisy Durham was still out there somewhere, wondering if his wife was still in the Durhams' kitchen finding chores for herself, wondering what had really happened to the kid and when she would surface. Then he dug a matchbook out of his pocket, lit the cigar, and sat back to enjoy the ride. He and Royman were going to make sixty bucks off this stash, enough for each of them to buy a fishing boat or put a down payment on a new car. *Sixty bucks off the slobs and the drunks and even the Jews*, he thought with a smile.

———

On Danforth Street, Victor sat in his parked car, crumbling Gus' list of Jewish businesses. Besides Pool's Dry Goods, he'd searched the tailor's place, a dental office, a men's suit shop, a doctor's office, a dress boutique, a stationer's, and a fruit and vegetable shop. The accused all cooperated, except for the dentist, Dr. Grunbaum, who submitted only after Victor threatened to arrest him. By the end of it all, Victor hadn't gained a scrap of evidence and had lost several precious hours—it was the middle of the night already. He considered Gus' idea of searching the Jews' homes, but no, that would take too long. Then he decided that maybe their preacher could provide some answers.

If Victor tried the rabbi's house, he wouldn't have found

him there. Rabbi Abrams had been at the temple since mid-afternoon, sitting in the sanctuary, worshipping and writing his Yom Kippur sermon. He knew nothing about what was happening, and so he worked undistracted under the perpetual light over the Torah ark.

———

When the clock on the dresser said 2:30, Jack turned out the light and lay down on his parents' bed. He stared into the blackness, listening to Martha's breathing and Harry's tossing. He never expected to fall asleep, but somewhere along the line, with Martha curled up next to him and Harry in a nest of blankets on the floor, he slipped beneath the surface of wakefulness.

Jack might have stayed in that light slumber, but all at once his mother's chickens squawked. He jerked to attention. The birds always fussed like this whenever the neighbor dog Agatha came scratching around the coop, and it didn't usually faze him. But tonight was different. *Tonight it might not be Agatha. Someone might be creeping around. Should I go take a look? What time is it, anyway?*

Fortunately, the birds quieted themselves after a few seconds, and all was silent again—no voices, no footsteps, just a faint yap from Agatha and the rustling of Harry's blankets.

Jack rolled from his side to his back. *Where were Mama and Pa sleeping? Did they make any more phone calls? Had anyone found Daisy?*

No, if Daisy had been found alive, word would have spread. Someone would have called the Pools, and everyone would have been sent to their own bedroom. But here they all were, sleeping—or not sleeping—in the wrong rooms. Things were still bad.

Jack got up. He picked up the *shofar* from the rocking chair and sat down, turning the horn over and over in his hands. For thousands of years, the Jews had used the *shofar* to ring the alarm of war, to panic the enemy in battle, and to herald the coming of peace. Over the eons, not one change had been made to the instrument's design. The sound Jack made on his *shofar* earlier tonight was the same sound made by his most ancient ancestors, ancestors who survived hate and cruelty over and over. *I come from a people who survive*, he told himself. *That has to count for something.*

Turning toward the window, Jack resolved to stay up and watch for the first hints of daylight to slide over the rooflines. What he'd do then, he had no idea. He only knew he had to do something, and if standing guard for daybreak was all he could manage, then so be it. Maybe he'd close his eyes first, though, just for a few minutes.

When he pried his eyes open, he thought he saw dawn breaking yellow and green low in the sky. It was a paltry smudge of light poking from a single corner of the horizon, as if the sun had sent a timid little substitute in its place. Jack wiped some of the condensation off the window and looked again at the patch of peculiar light gleaming through the glass.

But this wasn't the sun's first light. This was the temple. There was no mistaking the green-yellow glow spilling out of the synagogue's stained windows. There was no other color like it in the world. But why would the *shul* be lit up this time of night? Was it a fire—did someone set the building on fire? Were they after the rabbi? *What should I do?*

Jack slid out of the rocking chair, tiptoed across the room and down the hall, and grabbed his shoes out of his bedroom. But as soon as he returned to the hallway he bumped into Harry.

"What?" Jack whispered.

"Huh?" Harry yawned. "Martha just woke up. She wants her doll."

"Go back to bed and I'll get the doll. Tell Martha I'll bring it right now."

Harry nodded sleepily and stumbled back to his bed of blankets while Jack went on to Martha's room. His parents were there, one on Martha's bed and the other on the trundle bed. One of them was snoring. He hurried to the vanity table where Martha kept her toys. No one stirred.

Harry and Martha were sound asleep when he set the rag doll down on the rocker. The *shofar* caught his eye. He picked it up and tucked it into the waistband of his trousers. He padded down the stairs, stopped himself in time to catch the screen door before it slammed behind him, and then he started running.

The night was such a strange shade of black—dark enough to hide people who might be looking for him but pale enough, it seemed, to utterly expose him. *Are those voices? What's poking my side?—uh, the* shofar. He crossed Main Street. *Is that someone up ahead? Can people hear the sound of my breathing?* He turned onto Hill Street, and the temple came into view.

No flames, no fire truck. *Thank God.* But the trooper's police car was there, parked in front.

Edging through the temple doors and into the foyer, Jack could hear voices in the sanctuary. *I can't just walk in. It might not be safe. Where can I hide?* To his right there was a small coat closet. A few feet beyond that were the stairs leading up to the classroom. *Doesn't one of the stairs creak?* He hesitated, then slipped into the closet and shut the door behind him.

It smelled as musty as it did a decade ago when he used to hide with his Hebrew-school friends and make his mother "find" him. He'd forgotten all about those days. The closet was big and welcoming then. Tonight it was cramped and black and hung with stale air. Worst of all, it muffled the voices in the sanctuary. He opened the door a crack, just enough to hear.

"No, I have not heard anything about a little girl," the rabbi was saying. "How can I help you?"

"What do you know about Daisy Durham?" asked the unmistakable voice of the cop.

"I'm not familiar with this child. How old is she?"

"Four. Listen, I'll get right to the point, Father—"

"*Rabbi* Louis Abrams. And you are...?"

"Victor Brown."

"You are new," the rabbi said.

"That's right. Now, I need to ask, do you have a holiday coming up?"

"Yom Kippur begins with the next sundown."

"Is it a serious day, a fast day?"

"The most serious day of the year. Our Day of Atonement. But you came about a child. She is missing?"

"Since early afternoon."

"How could a thing like that happen? Wasn't anyone with her, so young?"

"We don't have too many answers just yet. Anyhow, look, I see you're getting ready for your holiday, and I'm curious about something. Do your holiday customs ever call for, you know, sacrifices?"

"Ah," said the rabbi in a scholarly tone. "In ancient times, our people did offer their animals—sheep, cattle, goats—at the Holy Temple in Jerusalem. But the Holy Temple was destroyed almost two thousand years ago. No animals have been offered since."

"Uh *huh*. Well, what about other kinds of sacrifices? Besides livestock."

"Other kinds? You mean fruits and vegetables?"

"Like humans."

"Where did you get such ideas?" the rabbi asked.

The calm in the rabbi's voice stunned Jack. It sounded like he was almost amused. *But of course he's calm. He doesn't know about the accusations or the searches or the broken window or the angry crowds. He thinks the trooper is just curious. And stupid.*

"I would like to set your sources straight," the rabbi said pleasantly.

"Yeah, okay, so about the girl—" Victor said.

"Yes, of course. We digress. I am happy to help you however I can."

"Good. Because I hear you people use the blood of a child for your holiday here. And with Daisy Durham missing, I have to wonder."

There was silence as the rabbi put together the threads of conversation—missing child, religious practices, animal sacrifices. Finally, in a much too quiet voice, he asked, "Are you accusing us of murder?" And then, releasing the muzzle on his anger, he roared, "How dare you invade our temple for this mockery?"

Jack dropped his head against the closet wall.

"Now, Father, let's try to keep calm," Victor said. "It's my duty to conduct a thorough investigation. So just answer the question: do you make human offerings?"

"Nothing could be more unthinkable! We do not murder."

"But do you use blood to—"

"Blood? Never! We even remove the blood from our meat. It takes salt and time, but we do it because the Bible—your Bible and mine—tells us to 'be steadfast in not eating the blood, for the blood is the life, and thou shalt not eat the life with the flesh.' We would rather go hungry than consume blood."

"Well then," Victor said, "why did—"

"Blood accusations," the rabbi broke in. "I should not be surprised in Troky, my Lithuanian home. I should not be surprised in much of the world. But in America? America is supposed to be a refuge from such madness. I would not have believed it possible here."

The rabbi drew a heavy breath and continued, "Sir, let me tell you why we wear canvas sneakers on Yom Kippur instead of our usual shoes. Because our shoes are made of leather. An animal had to die to fashion them. Yom Kippur is a day of special grace and compassion. You defile it with your accusations, and you disserve this little girl."

"Think what you like, Father. I'm still going to—" But Victor never got a chance to finish his sentence.

"Get him! Move it, move it!" The voices burst through the temple doors. "Show yourself, Abrams! It's all over now! Where've you got her? ABRAMS!" they yelled as they charged across the entrance.

The mob crowded into the sanctuary and started bellowing at both the rabbi and the trooper. "Give us the girl!"

"Make the murderer hand over the child!" "You'll burn for this!" "Take him in or we'll take him for you!" "Pig!" "Hang the damned butcher!"

Rabbi Abrams spoke before the trooper did. "Shame on you all!" he thundered. "You should be out searching for the lost child, or at home with your own families at such an hour. Leave! Do you hear me? Leave this holy place!"

A boy growled something as he approached the rabbi, but one of the men called him back. "He's pitch black on the inside, son. Keep your distance."

Another boy said something to the first one. His voice sounded a little like George Lingstrom's. Then the shouting began again.

———

Emaline, Lydie and Mrs. Durham sat in the kitchen with three untouched Coca-Cola bottles on the table. The radio was still playing from earlier in the night, and the local announcer was reading from *The World Almanac*. "Listeners, we've reached the wee hour of four o'clock, so I'll close tonight's broadcast with one last fascinating fact..." Emaline got up and jiggled the tuner. She found the Potsdam station and sat back down. "...a chicken in every pot and a car in every garage," Herbert Hoover was promising.

"Think he'll be our next President?" Lydie asked.

"Well, if he is," Emaline answered absently, "I guess we'll all be getting free automobiles and chicken dinners, won't we?"

After Hoover's campaign plug came a staticky rendition of "Button Up Your Overcoat," followed by the day's news. *The Yankees clinched the pennant today. A machine called an iron lung*

made its debut at Boston Children's Hospital; a girl who'd stopped
breathing recovered within seconds of being placed in the chamber.
Volunteers rescued nine more survivors— three of them children—
from last week's hurricane in Florida. The first successful helicopter
flight over the English Channel happened this afternoon. Then a
new Al Jolson song came on.

Emaline glanced at her mother, who was staring out the
window, and then she stood up.

"Going to try to sleep?" Mrs. Durham asked.

"No, I just—I have to get something upstairs. I'll be back."
She was gone for only a minute. "All right, Ma," she said when
she returned, holding a small paper bag. "I made something
for your birthday, but I think you should have it now. Here, it's
for good luck." She set the bag in front of her mother and sat
down beside her.

"For me? For my...? Oughtn't we wait?"

"No, Ma. Do it now. Go on."

Mrs. Durham picked up the paper bag, uncurled the
folded top, and withdrew a handmade bracelet strung with
red beads. She ran her fingers over the polished pieces of glass
as if they were her rosary. Red was Daisy's favorite color, the
color of her Raggedy Ann doll's hair, the color of her woolen
scarf—the one she didn't bring with her when she left the
house today. Red was the color of her dead husband's hunting
jacket. The color of the poppies that grew wild on the edge of
Paradise Woods. The color of blood.

"It's beautiful," she said at last. "So elegant."

"And the thing is, it's good luck—look." Emaline reached
over and flipped around the largest bead. On its back, she'd
glued a golden speck. "It's a mustard seed. We learned about it in

Sunday school. 'If you have faith as a grain of mustard seed—' "

" '—nothing shall be impossible unto you,' " Mrs. Durham finished. "The Book of Matthew?"

"That's right. Now put it on."

So she did. She'd do anything for some good luck.

———

The vicious cries stabbed Jack's ears. "Get 'im, fellows!" someone yelled. Another man called out, "They're bloodthirsty perverts, all of 'em!" Then the others shouted all at once.

Jack stepped out of the closet, moving almost without thinking. Hugging the wall, he inched toward the sanctuary and reached his hand around the doorframe. When he found the switch plate, he flipped it off and every light went out.

The temple blackened, and the shouts exploded into a hellish uproar. Jack pulled the *shofar* from his waistband and sounded a long, piercing blast into the darkness—one long, urgent note that said, *Now it's your turn to be afraid.*

Blinded men and boys were pushing, shoving, swearing. *Run, Rabbi Abrams*, Jack silently pleaded. *Hide. Do something, anything. Now!*

There was nothing more Jack could do. The darkness would either protect the rabbi or it wouldn't. He crept back into the closet, angry tears stinging his cheeks, feeling as small as a five-year-old hiding in the coat closet after Hebrew school—and much more helpless.

"Everyone hold it!" Victor hollered above the bedlam, flashlight in hand. "Everybody out, now! Out!"

"Go on," Victor ordered again. "Get yourselves home, all of you." He lit a path through the sanctuary and across the foyer, and the crowd filed out slowly. *Like kids being dragged out of a carnival before all the fun is over.* As the last straggler exited, the trooper stood in the doorway and announced, "I'm issuing a curfew till daybreak. That's for all of you. Until the sun's up, clear?"

"But I got animals to feed," one man said.

"And I gotta be at the plant at six," another added.

Victor shrugged. "You shoulda been asleep long ago, then. The curfew stands."

More grumbling. The gang didn't disperse until Victor threatened to extend the curfew until 8 a.m.

The temple door slammed shut, and the flashlight beam swept past Jack again. Then the trooper found the light switch. "Hey, where'd you go?" he asked from the back of the sanctuary.

Nothing.

"Mr. Abrams, they're gone."

Silence. Then the sound of something being pushed against carpeting. "I am here," came the rabbi's voice. "I took cover behind my lectern."

"Lookit, just let me take a look around, and I'll give you a ride home after."

"Please be quick about it," the rabbi said.

He thinks it's all over. Rabbi Abrams thinks this is the beginning and the end of the whole ordeal. Jack wanted to run to him and blurt out the whole story, but he had to get out of the temple before Victor got to the closet. So, while the trooper poked around the Torah scrolls and peered under the benches, he slipped outside and hoped he'd make it home before anyone realized he was gone.

It was 4:30 a.m. when the knock came. Emaline, Lydie
and Mrs. Durham had retreated to the living room, where
they nestled under the quilts and sank into the bottomless
sofa cushions. They weren't asleep, but the harsh thump of
knuckles against wood seemed to wake them just the same,
and they jumped up in a tangle of blankets and dread. Anyone
coming at this hour had to be bringing news.

They weren't sure they wanted to know what it was, and
they hesitated. The knock came again, harder this time.

Emaline went to the door and opened it slowly. She fully
expected to see the trooper, but it was George Lingstrom
who stood there instead, flushed, vaguely smiling, with his not
quite blond, not quite brown hair shielding his blue eyes.

"George?" Emaline said. "Why George, I thought—
come in."

"I saw your light on, so I figured you were up," he said.
When Emaline didn't reply, he continued, "I hope that's okay."

"Yes, yes, we've been up all night," Emaline said. "Do you
have news, George? Do you have anything to tell us?" She
didn't invite him to sit down. She didn't think of it. George
must have something important to say, she figured, or why
would he be here at this hour?

George brushed back his hair. "I guess I really just wanted
to stop by. See how you're doing. Find out what I can do."

"Well, you might as well come in and sit down," Mrs.
Durham said, motioning him to the love seat.

Emaline returned to her spot between her mother and

Lydie. "Honestly, George, if you really want to help, you could go to the woods and search for Daisy."

George sat up straighter. He seemed confused. "The woods? But..." He glanced at Lydie and Mrs. Durham. "The woods?"

"Yes, George, the woods," Emaline said. "That's where Daisy got lost. In the woods right in back of the house. You didn't know?"

George's lips wavered, as if he couldn't decide whether to smile or frown. "You said lost, but you mean...you mean kidnapped, right?"

This made Mrs. Durham's eyes fill, and she covered them with her hand. Lydie was about to say something, but Emaline spoke first. "What are you talking about, George?"

"The Jews, Emaline. Jack Pool. Everyone knows it—I figured you did too. Jack snatched her so they could...could..."

"Could what?" Emaline asked.

"Maybe I shouldn't say."

Mrs. Durham lowered her hand. "Don't listen to him," she whispered.

"No, I want to hear it. You think Jack took her so they could what?"

George looked to Mrs. Durham for help, but she offered none. "So they could bake her blood in their holiday bread."

Emaline's mouth fell open. "Jack? People think Jack...?"

"A bunch of us went to their church a while ago," George rushed on. "We were trying to get their preacher. You know, get him to tell us where they've got Daisy. But, well, it didn't go the way we planned."

"What was your plan?" she asked.

"Well, I was gonna...we were..."

"You were going to hurt him."

"Not necessarily. Not if he 'fessed up right away. Not if Daisy was still all right."

Emaline stood up. "Please go home."

"Em—"

"I'll see you out," she said, heading to the door, but George didn't get up. "Please," Emaline said. Her voice was determined even as it quavered.

Finally, George got up and went to the door, his face a grey shade of disappointment. "I was only trying to lend a hand. I thought I was helping you."

"Just go," she said faintly.

He stepped out onto the porch and then turned around to face her. "Em, I—"

Emaline closed the door. She stood there with her hand on the knob for a long time after his boot steps faded away. Then she turned the bolt and returned to the sofa, where she sank to the very bottom of the cushions.

SUNDAY, SEPTEMBER 23, 1928

It was 5 a.m. and Rabbi Abrams was home at last. He sat down at his kitchen table to rewrite his sermon. He lined up his fountain pen, ink bottle and legal pad, uncertain what to do with them. Everything was different now. He'd have to tell everyone what happened at the temple, and he'd have to do it in a meaningful way, a useful way, a way that would foster hope, not panic. But how?

He picked up the pen and stared at the blank sheet. Somehow the lines on the paper didn't look right. "I must be tired," he mumbled. He blinked several times and stared harder. The lines were quivering. He blinked again. Now the lines were fluttering like threads in the wind. No, not like threads—like ripples of water. Like sewer water.

Suddenly he was fourteen and in Lithuania, back in the Jewish ghetto of Troky, standing on a street corner. That was all he could do at first—stand there and wonder what all the shouting on the next street was about. Only when he heard the first death wail did he understand. He bolted home, praying that there was a home to go to.

With guns and torches, the raiders flooded the Jewish quarter and smashed the men's skulls, raped and drove nails through the heads of the women and children, burned down homes and stores, piled the dead in the streets, and then shot them full of bullets for good measure. Almost no one survived except for Louis' family. For two days they huddled underground in the freezing, filthy sewer waters beneath Troky, listening to the fire blasts overhead, eating and drinking nothing, seeing no other life, only sewer rats.

When the noise finally stopped, Louis, his parents and his two sisters crawled out of the sewer. As soon as he saw what had happened outside, he wanted to crawl back in. Babies lay slit like fish in their mother's arms. Men, flayed or burned crisp, made grotesque statues propped against fences and walls. Girls lay naked with pools of blood caught between their legs.

There was no point bothering to check on their cottage; everything was destroyed. But when his nose numbed to the rotting flesh, young Louis did stumble around the *shtetl* for a while, saying silent good-byes to the friends and neighbors who were now corpses.

At one point, Louis saw a child's hand reaching out from a wreckage of clapboards, unable to break free. He bent down and found a small girl hunched under the pile of wood.

"It's all right. They're gone now," he whispered to her. He took her hand, thin and cold. But the hand was all he got. It had been severed just above the wrist, and the blood oozed onto his foot. He fell on his knees and vomited.

Louis' older sister found him and helped him up. There was nothing to do now except stay alive. That meant getting as far away as possible from this place that had been home. So he and his family started walking. They walked, rode trains and hitchhiked across Europe, ending up hungry and exhausted in Wales. They'd trekked almost 1,500 miles, but for Louis the journey was just beginning. Traveling alone this time, he took a boat to New York City where he could live with a cousin, prepare for rabbinical school, and start a life in America.

Back in the ghetto, the rabbi wasn't able to help his people or even that one little girl. But today, he thought, maybe he could help both a lost girl and his community. Maybe he could organize a search party to look for Daisy Durham.

Pushing aside his writing materials—that would have to wait—he wondered who he should phone and whether he should wait until a more reasonable hour of the morning.

The telephone jolted him. He hoped it was the trooper calling to say that Daisy was found wandering the woods or a back road—and perhaps even to apologize. Then again, it could be one of his congregants calling. Someone may have passed away in the night—maybe old Max Clopman or poor Sadie Gelman, who was so sick. Yes, it was probably a death; anything else could wait until a sensible hour. He picked up the receiver.

"Rabbi, it's Sam Pool."

"Sam, what's wrong? It's not Eva, is it? Or one of the children?"

"No, it's—I'm sorry if maybe I wake you. Since last night I try to call. I need to tell you—do you know a girl is missing? Daisy Durham?"

"Why, yes. I was just thinking about her. I'm glad you called. We should help. I would like us to help look for her."

Silence, then a long exhalation.

"Sam, are you there? I was saying we should help find the girl."

"Rabbi, we cannot."

"Why not?" he asked, but even as he did, a groundswell of alarm flooded his insides. "We'll walk the streets or the schoolyard or—"

"Louis, listen to me. They say we murdered her. Us. The Jews."

Jack, listening in on his father's end of the conversation, was surprised to hear Mr. Pool speak so frankly, after his mother's cryptic words last night.

The rabbi could not respond. "But..."

"Louis?"

"How do you know this?" the rabbi asked.

And so Mr. Pool revealed everything that went on during the night. He told Rabbi Abrams about the interrogations, the store searches, the threatening crowds, the shattered window. "So we cannot go looking for the child. Outside, we shouldn't be. It isn't safe. Not after all that has happened and might happen still, you see?"

The rabbi wanted to say that no, he didn't see. But he did see, very well. He saw that all of this had happened without his even knowing about it, much less doing anything about it.

"Louis, I know this is —"

"Sam, there's more. They came to me too. At the synagogue. I just got home."

"Oh my God. They got you? What...how?"

"First the trooper barged in, saying he wanted to make a search. Then a gang forced its way in, shouting and drunk and trying to get their hands on me."

"Their *hands* on you?"

"I really thought they were going to lynch me. They had bloodlust in their eyes and in their voices. They wanted me dead, I think, or at least hurt. I thought it was the end for me. And then a miracle. The lights went out. All that wiring trouble we've been having, it saved me. I had a chance to hide.

"And then another miracle, a second one," the rabbi continued. "Don't ask me how, but out of nowhere a *shofar* blasted—I swear it. It scared the mob worse than the darkness did, and the trooper was finally able to get a hold of them. Kicked them out. But he searched the *shul* just the same. Even the ark he stuck his nose in, like we might have stuffed a body in there after we took the blood."

"My God," Mr. Pool murmured.

"I'm going to call the American Jewish Committee right after the Yom Kippur fast," the rabbi said. "They should be informed, and maybe they can help us. I'll phone them first thing. Meanwhile, I have to figure out what to say to everyone at services."

"We ought to cancel services," Mr. Pool said, "for our own good."

"Absolutely not! We must not cower. We will pray for ourselves and for the lost child."

"Louis, listen to me. They call us murderers—cannibals, even. They take over our *shul* and our stores. You, they almost drag away. With this kind of trouble, we should walk the streets and gather together? I say no."

The rabbi said nothing.

"Louis?"

"I trust I will see you here for *shlug kapporus* in a few hours. We need you. We need each other."

"I don't know. I will think it over, and do what is best for my family."

"As you should. Goodbye."

———

Mrs. Pool caught Jack eavesdropping on Mr. Pool's phone call with the rabbi. "Jack," she said, passing him on her way to the kitchen, "since you're up, feed the chickens, will you? And bring in the eggs if there are any. I think we'll bring the red hen for *shlug kapporus*, so make sure she's not all dusty."

Jack didn't know how his mother had revived her cool, but he wasn't going to be the one to tell her that Mr. Pool was talking about skipping services altogether. Instead, he grabbed his jacket from the stair rail and headed out the back door, relieved that no one seemed to know he'd been out during the night.

The sun perched on the treetops, just below the silver swaths of sky. This could have been any morning, any autumn sky, except that the air was filled with the stench of last night's violence, and maybe also the stink of what was yet to happen. *Anything could happen. At any moment. To any of us.*

As Jack walked down the porch steps, he caught sight of the neighbor dog, Agatha, sniffing around the coop. She was unusually excited, whining, poking her nose through the wire fence, wagging her tail, and finally letting out an eager yelp. Something was different. He ran to the coop.

The hens were dead. Headless, every one of them. Someone had slit their throats and tossed their faces into the egg bucket, except for one that was stuck on top of the fence. That head belonged to the red hen, the one Martha called Sunny, the one Mrs. Pool wanted to bring to *shlug kapporus*, the one that was supposed to be cooked into a meal for Frenchie LaRoux. Sunny's eyes were open, looking neither afraid nor angry, looking nothing at all—except dead. A trickle of blood made a crooked line from her beak down to the bottom of the fence, where Agatha was happily licking and scraping. Now Jack understood the late-night commotion in the coop, the sudden squawking followed by sudden quiet. It was a Jew-hater, not a dog, who'd trespassed.

Jack wondered for a second what note Sunny had made

with her last breath—low C, high A? Was it an oscillating vibrato, or maybe a sliding glissando? Then he raced to the garage for a shovel.

He half expected to find the car tires slashed, as well, but they were all right. He lowered the shovel from the wall rack and walked the perimeter of the Model T to make sure nothing was ripped off or smashed. As he did, an impulse gripped him—a powerful urge to take the car and plow it straight into the Sit Down Diner. Jack hated Gus and his cronies. He hated everyone who had, or might have had, a part in any of this, and he wanted them to pay. But there was no time to dream of revenge. He had to get rid of the chickens.

Jack let himself into the coop and began digging a hole. He didn't want his mother to see the butchery, so he worked fast. He dug and dug, his hands burning against the wooden handle. *Blisters*, he thought. *Just what I need on top of my cut. Blisters on my fingering hand and blisters on my bowing hand.*

He kept digging, and with each scoop of cold black soil he felt himself harden. *Is this what being a Jew gets me? Is this my reward for studying Torah and keeping kosher and missing every single baseball game?* He wasn't just mad at the Jew-haters anymore. He was mad at God. *How could You let this happen?*

Jack hit something hard with the tip of his shovel and crouched to remove the offending rock. He threw it over the fence, startling Agatha enough to make her dart back a few feet. He considered tossing her a chicken head; then maybe she'd go away. Better yet, maybe she'd bury it in her master's garden, and he'd dig it up with his bulbs. He'd finger it curiously, stroking away the dirt, thinking it was a misshapen bulb, and then when he saw what it really was, he'd drop it like a snake, revolted. Agatha's master could be one of them, after all. Anybody could be one of them, anybody at all. There was no way to be sure.

Jack went on digging, stabbing at the ground. He felt like his arms would break. He dug mechanically, almost violently, until the hole was deep enough. Then he threw the snarl of bloody carcasses in and began covering the grave.

The hole was scarcely half filled when Mrs. Pool's voice jolted him from behind. "Jack, what's taking you so long?" she asked. Without thinking, he turned around to face her.

She blanched when she saw the bloody shovel and his bloodstained hands. "Jack, what...happened?" She suddenly winced at the smell. Agatha took a step toward her, tail wagging.

"I didn't want you to see," Jack said.

Mrs. Pool was as wide-eyed as the dead chickens. She breathed in the dirt and the carnage, looking like she might get sick, looking like an older and more fragile version of herself. "You finish up here, then," she said briskly. "I'll need to call Mrs. Silver to see if she can bring the bird this time. Get rid of the feathers too. And don't tell your father, not yet. He doesn't want us to go as it is."

Jack watched his mother brush past Agatha and lift her skirt as she climbed the back steps. Her writing pad slipped out of her apron pocket, and she bent to pick it up. When all this was over, Jack knew she would scribble the story down in that pade. He wondered how it would all end.

——

The Sit Down Diner buzzed nonstop all morning. Joe Runions said he saw the Jewish tailor carrying a particularly long pair of shears last week. Picky Willard chimed in that the Jewish doctor bought a bottle of ether at the apothecary the other day, and Cecilia Gardener said she noticed a truck delivering a box the size of a small coffin to Popkin's Furniture the day before. Later, old man Claghorn said he heard all about the store searches from his cousin Bernie.

"Some folks took a look inside their church too," Chuck Petru said. "Didn't go so well, I hear. But they say they heard a trumpet in there, like an angel's horn, like a sign from the Lord Himself, saying justice must be served. So it's not over yet."

Just before noon, Stretch Spooner, one of the factory foremen, came in for his regular lunch. He took his regular stool and his regular cup of coffee and, as usual, he set his walking stick right on the counter. Everyone knew the walking stick was hollow; he kept it filled with liquor, so a swig was as nearby as a screw of the handle.

"Saw the queerest thing this morning," Stretch said. "I was reading the paper and happened to glance out my window, the one that looks out on their preacher's backyard. And what did I see?"

Everyone leaned in.

"I saw a circle of Jews. And inside that circle? The preacher dancing all over and singing and waving a goddamn chicken around. A live one. Like something you'd read about in the *National Geographic* or something." He drained the creamer into his cup while the others murmured.

"Hold on now, that's not all," Stretch said. "When that preacher finally stops trotting around the circle, he takes the bird over to this big box he keeps in the yard, and when he comes back into sight, the chicken's head is missing. Gave me the heebie jeebies, I tell you. I locked the whole house right up after I saw that show."

The diner grew mute.

"Savages," Buzzy Degon finally said from the counter. "Well, sooner or later the truth will come out. Then they'll get theirs."

"Stop already," said his wife. "Someone's gonna find the little girl."

"What's left of her," Buzzy said, toying with his sugar doughnut. "Let's just hope it's nobody faint-hearted."

Gus just smiled.

"Why did the chickens all fly away?" Martha had her face pressed to the dining room window. Her hair was still wet from her morning bath, and the back of her neck was prickled with goose bumps. Jack stood behind her, not knowing what to say. "Is that why Mama didn't want to go to the rabbi's?" she asked. "Because of the chickens?"

Jack lifted a hand to her bony shoulder. "Mama's sad about the birds," he said, "just like we are. She doesn't feel like going anywhere. So we're going to stay home. For now."

"Oh." The word dampened the window. "But why did the chickens go away? Harry told me chickens can't fly. I knew he was wrong. I wanted to make a roof for them, for the coop, to keep them in, and he told me I didn't need to. He's such a stupid liar."

"Am not," said Harry, staggering sleepily into the room, at which point Jack shot him a glare. "Just because I was wrong doesn't make me a liar. Besides, if you'd built that roof, the chickens couldn't have flown off to look for Daisy."

Martha peered at Harry with a mixture of interest and suspicion.

"Haven't you ever heard of homing pigeons?" Harry asked, dropping into the captain's chair at the head of the table. "They go out and look for things or deliver messages or do whatever their trainers want them to do. Birds are smarter than you think. And I'm pretty sure those chickens are gliding around the sky, looking for Daisy."

Martha looked up at Jack, but he wouldn't look back. Then she walked over to Harry and put her fists on his knees, eyeing him, trying to decide whether to believe him. "Will they come back when they're done looking?" she finally asked.

"Maybe," Harry said. "Maybe they'll come straight back to live inside a fence where people steal their eggs and dumb dogs scare the feathers off them. Or maybe they'll decide they like their freedom and stay out in the wilderness. Maybe they'll decide to live in Paradise Woods with the other critters, for all we know. That wouldn't be so bad, would it?"

Martha considered this question solemnly. She climbed into Harry's lap and examined his face. He looked right back at her. "Can we get more chickens if they don't come back?" she asked.

"Definitely," Harry said. "Anyways, I'm hungry. Let's go see if there's any *challah* left." He took her hand and led her to the kitchen.

———

Emaline was tired of answering the door. Actually, she was just plain tired. She never went back to sleep after her bad dream. How could she, with all that dread whirling round her head? She was afraid for Daisy, terrified of what might have happened to her. She was worried about her mother. And now she couldn't stop thinking about Jack, agonizing about what he must be going through. All she wanted was to be left alone, but even that was too much to ask for.

Today since sunup, a steady stream of well-wishers had come by to drop off more food. By mid-morning, Mrs. Durham had resorted to taking a sleeping pill, one of the pills left over from the crushing insomnia following her husband's death. Now she was sleeping right through the incessant knocking and chatting, so it was up to Emaline to answer the door.

"I don't think I can look one more person in the eye and tell them I'm okay," Emaline told Lydie as they sat in the kitchen with their beads. "Why does everyone keep asking me how I am? I'm horrid, that's how I am. Can't people see that their smiles and their greeting-card wishes only make it worse? Can't they give me a little privacy instead of casseroles?"

One of the earliest callers this morning had been Mrs. Lingstrom. She brought a jar of peaches she'd put up over the summer. Emaline thought George's mother looked a little ill or might even have been crying. She didn't mention it, though—she didn't want to get into a conversation. She was just relieved that George wasn't with her. She couldn't face him, not right now.

When the knock came shortly after noon, Emaline ignored it, hoping whoever it was would just leave their package on the steps and go. But a minute later, the knock sounded again. Reluctantly, Emaline got up and peeked through the lace curtains in the living room. "It's the Thompson twins," she whispered to herself. Vanessa Lee and Virginia Lou, from her class at school. Vanessa held a picnic basket on one arm, and both girls were smiling. Apparently, they didn't know that everything worth smiling about was gone.

Emaline didn't go to the door. Instead, she went back and sat with Lydie in the kitchen, resuming her beading despite the repeated knocking. "Pay no attention," she told her cousin. But the knocking only got louder.

"Let me get rid of them," Lydie said. She went to the door, bracing herself for the hard slap of the Thompson twins' cheerfulness.

"Hi, ladies," Lydie said. "I'm sorry it took me so long to answer. We were—"

"That's all right," Vanessa said brightly. "We've got something for Emaline." From the size of their basket, it was probably a complete supper. More food that would go uneaten.

"I'll take it to her," Lydie said.

"Oh, but we were really hoping to see her," said Virginia. "Just for a minute?"

"Good morning, Vanessa, Virginia," Emaline said, walking from the kitchen doorway to her cousin's side.

"Emaline," they cooed. One of them said, "You're all we've been thinking about. The only thing."

Emaline raised her arms to receive the basket, but instead of handing it to her, the twins stepped apart.

Behind them stood Daisy.

DAISY!

Daisy was back! Mud plastered her legs and arms, and a red trickle marred her chin, but she was alive and safe and very much home.

While Lydie shrieked, Emaline could only stare. Her eyes grew glassy and large, and her mouth trembled as her hands flew straight out to her sister. "Daisy!" she cried, crossing the threshold. She scooped her sister up and carried her inside, burying her face in the little girl's hair.

Daisy's golden eyes got wet, and she started to sob. Her knees, skinned and as filthy as if she'd spent the last twenty-four hours crawling on the ground, dug into Emaline's sides. The girls squeezed each other tightly, then tighter still, until Daisy gasped for breath.

"Thank God," Emaline sighed, rocking and twirling and looking like she was winding up to go airborne.

"Em," Daisy said through her tears. Her tangled hair smelled of grass. "Em, I got lost."

"I know," Emaline said, although that wasn't exactly true. She hadn't known whether Daisy was lost or stolen or dead.

When Emaline picked a few pieces of dried leaves from her sister's hair, Daisy winced, "Ouch!" and rubbed the back of her head.

Emaline felt Daisy's head. "Hey, you've got an egg here. What happened?"

"Dunno. I—don't remember."

"You're bleeding too," Emaline said, pointing to her chin, but when she wiped the red liquid, she found it was sticky and smelled sweet. "Cherry or strawberry?"

"Strawberry—licorice, from my friends," she said, craning around to see the twins.

"How'd you know I was lost?"

"Everyone knew, silly," Virginia said. "Everyone's been troubled sick over you."

Daisy frowned. "Is Mommy mad?"

"Of course not," Emaline assured her. "She's going to be very, very happy. I promise."

"I wanna see Mommy," she said, and then she started to cry again.

"I'll take you right upstairs to her. But Vanessa, Virginia, how—where—did you ever find her?"

"To tell the truth," Vanessa said, "we weren't actually looking for her. She found us. We were going to have a picnic over to the point after church." She raised her basket as evidence. "We'd just biked to the edge of the woods and were spreading out our meal, and there she was, right at our blanket. A little ragged and plenty hungry, but walking on two feet. All the way out to the point—imagine! She's got a couple pieces of my pie in her now."

Emaline tried to grasp Vanessa's words, but they were too crazy and mixed-up. "Daisy, Daisy," she asked, "what happened in those woods?"

Daisy shrugged. "I got lost. I couldn't get out. It was dark, and I couldn't get out." She shuddered and laid her head heavily on her sister's shoulder.

Lydie asked, "Didn't you hear the people out there hunting for you?"

"I hid," she said, " 'cause Mommy told me about strangers. I hid good. They went away. But then it was too dark. I had to wait till daytime to come out, and then I saw Virginia and Vanessa—and lots and lots of food."

"Were you scared?" Emaline asked.

"A little."

"Did you sleep at all?"

"I didn't have any dreams."

"Were you so cold in that bit of a coat?"

"A little."

Emaline ran her hand down the front of Daisy's coat. She could feel her ribs and her hard little belly through the fabric. At the pocket, something soft bulged out. She reached in and extracted, of all things, Daisy's underpants wadded into a ball. "Hey," Emaline said, "why aren't you wearing your panties?"

Daisy blushed. "I climbed over a fence with pointy things," she said, holding the panties up so Lydie and the twins could see the rip. "I'm thirsty."

"You come with me then," Emaline said. "We'll go see Ma and then you can have whatever you like all day long. But first, I think you owe our friends here a big thank you."

Daisy looked hard into Vanessa's face. She studied Virginia's poodle curls and faux pearl earrings. She opened her mouth as if to speak, but only yawned. Then she tightened her legs around Emaline, reached forward, and shut the door in the twins' face.

"Daisy," Emaline said, reaching for the door, "that's not nice."

"No!" Daisy pushed her sister's hand away from the knob and held the door closed until she heard the twins' footsteps going down the porch stairs. Then, when she was satisfied that the door wasn't going to fly back open, she relaxed. "I want Mommy."

Emaline carried her mud-crusted, tear-stained, candy-drizzled prize upstairs, with Lydie following. Daisy pushed open the bedroom door with one foot and then climbed down from her sister's arms and tiptoed over to the bed. Her mother was sleeping heavily, her pillow half off the bed and her rosary at her side.

"Mommy!" Daisy shouted. "Mommy, I'm home!"

Emaline had to go over and give her mother's shoulder a little shake. First one eye opened—slowly and with effort—and then the other. Mrs. Durham was still trying to focus her vision when Daisy jumped on her. "Mommy! Mommy!"

"Daisy?" she said quietly, very quietly, afraid of waking herself if this was only a wonderful dream. "Daisy! My darling!" She grabbed hold of Daisy and sobbed so hard the bed shook.

Emaline sat on the edge of the bed, rubbing the back of the little girl with the torn stockings and matted hair.

"I'll call Mother," Lydie said after a while. "Get her to tell the radio station and the police." But they didn't hear her.

When Lydie checked on them just before heading home, Daisy was nestled against her mother like an extra layer of skin, and Emaline had one arm tucked around her sister's waist. The three of them mirrored each other's deep-sleep breathing and held each other like they'd never let go.

—

It didn't take long for the good news to spread. At the Sit Down, Tiny the cook had just snapped on the radio when Daisy's return was first announced. He shouted through the pass-through for everyone to hear, "The girl's been found!"

His announcement was met with a dumbstruck hush.

"Dead or alive?" Gus called back to him.

"Safe and sound," he said, and then a sigh swept the diner.

Jed Pike, sitting with his wife at the far end of the counter, was the first to break the glad chatter that followed. "I'm not resting so easy," he said, biting into an apricot Danish. "No way."

The weight of his voice sucked the bliss right out of the room.

"Whaddya mean, Jed?" Gus pointed his cigar at him. "There still trouble?" He hardly cared about the answer, though. He'd gotten his liquor supply without a hitch, and that's all that really mattered. The liquor supply that was going to buy him a fishing boat or a Buick or maybe that trip to Lake Placid he'd always wanted to take.

"I still say those Jews had her," Jed said. "I bet they just let her go 'cause they knew they were about to get pinched. That's what I think, and you'd all be fools to think otherwise."

Before anyone could respond, the sleigh bells jangled, and Frenchie LaRoux walked in. "Morning, folks," he said, "or I guess it's afternoon. You hear the news?"

"Just," Gus said, pouring Buzzy Degon a refill on his coffee.

Frenchie took the last empty stool at the counter. "Didja hear the girl's panties were missing when they found her?"

Silence. Groans. More silence.

"Those pigs," Eaton Lorado spat. "Those dirty pigs. You know, they're gonna be hiding in that church of theirs all night tonight, thinking it's gonna blow over. Well, it's not, and they'd better pray for forgiveness while they're in there."

"Amen," said Jed, and he took another bite of his Danish.

———

Jack's necktie was too tight, so he kept tugging at it as he walked between Harry and his father, with Martha and his mother a few steps ahead. They were on their way to *Kol Nidre*, the evening Yom Kippur prayers. They moved fast and kept glancing behind them, even though the dirt roads were empty.

This was the first time they'd been out on the street since

last night. They'd spent the whole day waiting—waiting for the trooper to call the rabbi or stop by their houses and say it was a terrible mistake, waiting for Fred Dimock, editor of the *Massena Observer*, to ask them for a statement. They waited the whole afternoon, during their pre-fast meals, and into the evening, but there was nothing, and it made them wonder whether things really were all over.

Mrs. Pool held Martha tightly with one hand and checked her jewelry with the other. She'd never worn both her diamond brooch and her pearl necklace at the same time before, but Mr. Pool said he was worried about leaving the jewelry in an empty house tonight—an empty house with a piece of cardboard where the living room window belonged. As for Jack, he'd tucked his cello under his bedcovers, and now he wondered if he'd picked too obvious a hiding spot.

"Don't pull away from me, Martha," Mrs. Pool scolded.

"You're pinching my hand," Martha complained.

"I wouldn't have to pinch if you didn't pull."

Crossing Main Street, Jack looked over at the diner. Yellow light spilled out of the windows, and he could see the blue outlines of the customers inside. It was just another night to them, he supposed. They were eating their smoky meats and buttery potatoes and treating each other as if they were human beings. Maybe the trooper was in there too, yucking it up with the crowd. Maybe they were all having a good old time chatting about the look on Jack's face last night, about hurling eggs and rocks, about headless chickens. Or maybe they were having a serious talk in there, planning the next thing they would do to uncover the 'truth.' Jack kept walking.

At the synagogue, Rabbi Abrams was standing on the front

steps, greeting each family as they arrived. "Jack," he said, offering his hand. "I'm looking forward to hearing you blow the *shofar* tomorrow for us."

Jack took the rabbi's hand and tried to plumb his thoughts. *Does he know I was here last night?* Jack couldn't tell. The rabbi was either totally poker-faced or genuinely clueless.

Everyone came—the entire congregation—except for Simon Slavin, who was still in Albany trying to get his store door repaired long-distance, and the Popkins, who were with family in Watertown, and Sarah Gelman's mother, who was too sick.

"You showed," Jack's friend Abe Goldberg mouthed, taking a seat directly behind him. Jack nodded.

Old Max Clopman, holding his cane more tightly than usual, arrived with Benny Kaplan and took his regular place in the front row. Sarah Gelman entered soon after, wearing a beaded navy dress, her face half-hidden behind her dark curls. He nodded to her, but she didn't see.

The chanting began. Jack listened for a while to Rabbi Abram's rich voice intoning the ancient lyrics. Then he let his attention stray around the sanctuary. Everything was the same as ever: the women in grey or brown dresses, praying or quieting their daughters or whispering to each other. The men in their best suits doing the same alongside their sons. The same prayers in the same order with the same melodies.

He wanted it to be different.

How can anything stay the same when everything—the world, me, maybe even God – has changed? Jack wanted to make the Hebrew words and the music echo his bitterness. He wanted everyone to wear angry red or grieving black. He wanted lightning to sizzle through the windows and thunder to rattle the benches. He wanted some sign that the others felt the way he did, that they weren't just trying to forget what happened, that he wasn't alone.

He didn't get what he was looking for. When services ended, he walked home silently along the unlit streets and closed himself in his room. His cello was still there. He put it back on its stand and stretched out on the bottom bunk. A few threads hung from Harry's bunk above, and he swatted them absently.

"Why won't You do something?" he demanded out loud.

He listened for a long time for a reply. Then he fell asleep, still in his suit and tie, on top of the bedcovers.

MONDAY, SEPTEMBER 24, 1928

Jack was the first one up the next morning. In the bathroom, he splashed cool water on his face and combed his hair. Thirst had set in, and hunger would soon follow. He watched the water rush teasingly down the sink before turning off the faucet. Then he plodded down the stairs and lay on the living room sofa, where the brisk air seeped easily around the makeshift cardboard window. Even with his legs curled and his arms hugging his chest, he felt cold—not from the wind that grazed his face, but from somewhere deep inside.

With the sun still low in the east, everyone gathered again at temple. During the *Yizkor* memorial prayers, Jack stood on the outside steps and leaned against the wrought-iron railing. Martha skipped around the sidewalk with a pack of other kids, while Harry gathered with a few boys to talk. The handful of adults lucky enough to be outside kept track of the small ones, although they also seemed to be watching Jack.

Sarah Gelman sat on the small stoop and leaned against the building with her eyes closed. This would surely be the last *Yizkor* she'd spend outside; her mother, devastated by a stroke, hadn't been expected to last even this long. God was sealing the Book of Life today, and Mrs. Gelman was not going to be in it. This time next year, Sarah would be inside the synagogue, reciting the *Yizkor* prayer in memory of her mother.

Jack walked over to her. "Hi, Sarah."

Her eyes fluttered open. "Jack," she said, her lips parting into a smile. "How are you doing?"

He shrugged. "You?"

"Gus fired me today."

Jack's eyebrows rose.

"Well, he didn't actually tell me I was fired. He called this morning to say there was a change in the schedule, that he needed me to work today."

"On Yom Kippur?"

"And if I refused, I shouldn't bother coming in for my regular shift tomorrow."

Jack thought of Sarah, of how she looked the last time he saw her at the diner, running around in her hairnet and apron, her thin arms laboring under the heavy platters of food. He thought of how Gus had eyed her that day through the smog of his cigar—not looking at her face, but looking her up and down.

"You're better off away from that place," Jack said.

"I need the money, though."

"I'm sorry, Sarah. I'm really..."

"No, Jack, I didn't mean to blame—"

"All right," called Mendy Segal, throwing open the temple doors. "You can come back in now." Suddenly, Martha was at Jack's side, and Sarah was walking ahead with little Ruthie Black.

Jack kept his eye on Sarah. He'd never noticed how pretty she was, with her heart-shaped mouth, her vibrant green eyes, and milky swan's neck. Jack wondered why he hadn't ever noticed her this way before.

Because of Emaline, that's why.

———

The remaining hours of prayer and fasting passed slowly. People wandered in and out of the sanctuary. Mothers took home the children who were too young to fast, returning with them after lunch. People whispered with bent heads. Jack thought about water and food and whether his cello was safe. He wondered whether Emaline or Mrs. Durham would

phone—or if they'd already tried while the Pools were at *shul*.
Finally, in the late afternoon, Rabbi Abrams announced his
sermon, which meant that services were nearly over.

"I want to share a story with you," the rabbi began.

Jack settled back on the bench. He considered the rabbi's
talks—filled with colorful tales, both true and imagined—to
be the entertainment portion of the services.

"This is a story about a young man," the rabbi continued.
"A young man who risked his own safety to help another man."

The rabbi seemed to be looking straight at Jack as he
spoke. A twinge of something—he didn't know what, maybe
satisfaction, maybe relief—shot through him.

"This young man—let us call him...Buddy—was growing
up in a village much like ours. One evening, he was walking
home along the riverbank, his books in one hand, his baseball
bat in the other. Suddenly, he heard angry voices up ahead
in a wooded area. He ran toward the sound, and what did he
find? The village tailor pressed against a tree by the local stone
mason, who had a fist raised, ready to strike."

Jack pictured the rabbi being cornered by the pack right
here in the temple. Cornered by men with fists and maybe
guns, as well.

"Buddy dropped his books so he could wield his baseball
bat with both hands. 'Leave him alone!' he shouted, swinging
the bat and heading straight to the mason. Startled, the mason
let go of the tailor and ran away."

Jack hoped the fleeing mason got hit by a car as soon as he
reached the street. But it didn't matter. What mattered was
that the rabbi knew...didn't he?

"After thanking Buddy for his assistance, the tailor

walked over to a tree stump and carved these words with his pocketknife: 'Buddy helped me here.' Then he picked up a stick and wrote in the dirt. 'The mason hurt me here.'

"Buddy asked why the tailor wrote one message in wood, the other in dirt. The answer was simple, the tailor explained. 'I will never forget how you helped me. Anyone who passes this stump will also know about your kindness. But I want the memory of my quarrel with the stone mason to fade, just as the rain will wash out the words in the dirt.'"

Wait a minute, Jack thought uneasily.

Rabbi Abrams stepped out from behind the podium. "Today we ask God to forgive us our sins, yes. But today we also ask ourselves to forgive those who have sinned against us, those who have lied to us, violated us, spoken ill of us."

What? Jack couldn't believe what he was hearing. *Forgive?* The rabbi couldn't mean it.

But he did mean it. "How can we ask the Lord for forgiveness," the rabbi said, "if we won't forgive those who have hurt us?"

I'm not going to forgive the people who accused me of murder. I don't want to forgive them. I won't act as if yesterday didn't happen. I won't.

"Forgiveness may not take away our pain, but it will bring us closer to the Almighty," the rabbi said. "Just as He is merciful, so we should be merciful."

Jack tuned the rabbi out. It hurt him just to think about forgiving anyone. He thought instead of his Bentley interview—suddenly only a day away. Tomorrow morning he'd board the sunrise train, travel for hours through the Adirondacks and Finger Lakes, get off at the Syracuse station, and walk a mile to the music school. *I'd walk the whole way to Syracuse if I had to. I'd do anything to get out of here.*

Tomorrow Jack's father would reopen the store. He'd open his doors to all the Jew-haters and pretend everything was fine. He'd speak kindly to everyone, even though any of them could be the one who shot the rock through his living room window, who decapitated his hens, who accused his son of killing a little girl. The best Mr. Pool could hope for was that they'd play the same game and make believe nothing was different; business as usual was better than no business at all. It made Jack sick, and it made the Bentley School more necessary than ever.

Jack felt a poke in his ribs. "What is it?" he asked Harry irritably.

"The *shofar*," Harry whispered. "Rabbi's calling you up."

Jack had forgotten. His *shofar* was sitting beside him the entire service. Completely off guard, he took the horn and stood up. All eyes were on him. Everyone was counting on him—he could see it in their faces. They wanted him to breathe a clear and vital sound, a sound powerful enough to remind them that God breathed life and strength into them all.

Jack joined the rabbi on the *bima*, uncertain whether he could make any sound at all. *I'm not ready. I haven't practiced enough. I don't feel what I need to feel.*

As he raised the ram's horn, Jack saw his father smiling at him. His half-blind father was looking straight at him and smiling a proud smile. Jack pressed his lips against the *shofar*. He inhaled deeply and then forced the air out of his lungs, through his lips, and into the horn, doubting what would come out the other end.

A strong blast shot to the far walls of the sanctuary. One long blast—God reigned. Several short blasts—God reigns. Another long blast—God will reign forever. He lowered the *shofar*, a little dizzy from blowing and very relieved to be finished.

"On Yom Kippur," the rabbi read from the Torah, "you shall sound the horn throughout the land...and proclaim liberty unto all the inhabitants."

Liberty. Jack fell back into place next to Harry with that word echoing in his ears. *Syracuse.*

———

Jack didn't say much at the dinner table after Yom Kippur. He had nothing to say, plus he was busy shoveling his mother's *lokshen kugel*—brimming with noodles, fruit and sweet spices—into his mouth.

"May I be excused?" he asked when he finished his second helping.

"But there's dessert," his mother said. "Why don't you stay?"

"Jack has big day tomorrow," his father pointed out. "Let him go. He is excited."

"He looks more tired than excited," she said. "Okay, go."

Jack went to his room and practiced his audition piece over and over until Harry came in for bed. "Mama says go to sleep before you wear your fingers away," Harry said.

"Fine," said Jack, but he didn't stop playing.

While Jack worked and reworked one particularly difficult bar, Harry changed into his nightshirt and climbed into the top bunk. Then he reached over and tugged the pull string, turning the room black. "I think she meant now," he said, yawning.

Ten minutes later, Jack was lying awake in the bottom bunk, making the bedsprings grate as he turned from his back to his chest and then to his back again.

"What's eating you?" Harry asked.

"Nothing. I just...nothing."

"You nervous about your audition?"

"Sort of."

"Why? You practiced enough. Everyone says you're good."

"Being good isn't always enough. Some schools put quotas on Jews, y'know."

Harry swung his head over the railing. "What?"

"I hear even places like Harvard and Yale, if they think you're Jewish—"

"Says who?"

"Says a lot of people. I just never believed them, before now."

"Well, our name doesn't sound very Jewish, so you've got that going for you. Not like Abe Goldberg's or Eli Tennenbaum's."

"Yeah, well, maybe that's what the interview is for. To see if I look Gentile or not."

"Hmm," Harry said, lying back down. "You could always ask them where the nearest church is. Or if the school has a chapel choir you can join. Or if they serve fish on Fridays."

"Good night, Harry."

"What? Isn't Pa always telling us how our great-uncle in Russia dressed up like a woman when the Jew-hating army came to draft him? And how his grandmother pretended to be pregnant so she could—"

"Good night, Harry."

"I was just trying to help."

Jack tried to make out his cello in the shadows of the bedroom. Tomorrow he would play like his life depended on it. As far as he was concerned, his life *did* depend on it—because he didn't know how he'd survive if he had to stay here.

TUESDAY, SEPTEMBER 25, 1928

Jack tried sitting on the bench outside the train station, but he couldn't stay put, so he stood on the platform, his cello on one side and the ticket master's scrawny dog on the other. Over and over he checked to see if his ticket and wallet were still in his pocket. His mother was right, he realized. The brown shoes would have gone better with his pants and sweater than the black ones he ended up getting. Still, the oxfords were dressy enough, and the blisters that sprang up on his heels during the walk to the station hardly hurt at all.

He couldn't wait to get out of his house this morning. His mother was nervous and excited and even a little teary, as if she were sending Jack away for a year, not a day. She kept reminding him, as if he needed reminding, that he'd never taken the train by himself, or traveled to Syracuse, or been this far from home. She wanted to go with him to the station, but he said no, so instead she followed him around the house and issued orders to Mr. Pool until it was finally time to go.

Shielding his eyes against the shafts of early light, Jack surveyed the long strip of track, then rechecked his ticket, wallet and watch. *When will it get here?* He'd only make the interview on time if the train stayed on schedule. Showing up late would be tantamount to telling the dean he wasn't particularly interested. He had to be prompt. *Did I remember my comb?*

Jack was so deep in thought, he didn't hear the footsteps from behind, but suddenly the ticket master's dog was wagging its tail, and someone was standing next to him, breathing hard. Not *someone* as in anyone. *Someone* as in Emaline.

She wore a pale blue dress Jack had never seen on her before, white gloves, and the hat she'd bought at the store over the weekend, the black one with the silk rose. Jack looked down at his own clothes and stood up straighter. Jack thought he picked up the faint scent of perfume.

"Emaline," he said, his voice uneven.

"Hi," she smiled. The skinny dog ambled over to her and tapped her leg with its swishing tail.

"You traveling?"

"No—well, we're going to Waddington later to spend a few days with my Aunt Pearl. Ma thinks we all need a rest after—after the weekend. I wouldn't exactly call it traveling. Anyway, I was just at your house, and when your mother said you'd already left, I—"

"My house?"

She scratched the mutt's head and stepped closer to Jack. "I wanted to see you off, wish you good luck."

She remembered. "You didn't run all the way down here, did you?" Jack asked.

"In my Aunt Pearl clothes? No, Ma dropped me off. She and Daisy are having breakfast at the Sunflower."

God, she looks beautiful with the morning sun on her.

Emaline took another step closer, until her foot met his cello case. "Jack, I didn't come just to wish you luck. I came to say I'm sorry. So terribly sorry about this weekend."

"I..." Jack's head wobbled with questions. *What exactly is she sorry for—how much does she know? Does she know I was the one accused? That someone killed all our hens and left their heads for me to bury? That the temple was raided and the stores searched? Does she know Pa's afraid he won't have customers anymore? Or that Mama won't let Martha play in the yard by herself?* Jack had a thousand questions, but the one that came out was, "How did you hear?"

"Oh," Emaline sighed. "Well, I heard a little about it during our ordeal, and then my Aunt Clarisse filled me in after. You can't change your bloomers without Aunt Clarisse knowing about it. She knows everything, that woman."

But does she really?

"Why would anyone do such wicked things?" Emaline asked. "I feel like this is all my fault, all because I couldn't manage to get home for Saturday lunch on time." She turned her head away, and the movement let a ray of sun catch her necklace, a gold cross on a chain.

"It's not your fault." Jack tried to think of something else to say, but Emaline's pendant commandeered his attention. The crucifix. It's what stood between Emaline and him, like an electrified fence, all glittery and metallic and masquerading as jewelry.

"What are you looking at?"

"I, nothing. It's just, your necklace. It's...nice."

"This?" She held up the cross. "This is a crucifix."

"Oh. I mean, yes."

"My father gave it to me when I took my first communion, did I ever tell you that?"

She slid her fingers over the chain.

"No. I mean, maybe. Sorry, I didn't mean to make you—"

"It's fine, really."

Emaline glanced behind her to see if anyone was around. The ticket master was smoking a cigarette on the bench outside the station, but he was busy reading the paper, so she went ahead and touched his fingers. He clutched her hand fast and stared full-on into her topaz eyes. They didn't speak for a moment.

"Thanks for coming," he said at last. "I'll need all the luck I can get."

"I really shouldn't be wishing you any luck at all, you know. Why should I, when I don't want you to go?"

Jack's mouth opened a sliver.

"Look, I know you want—you need—to go," she said. "But the honest, selfish truth is, I don't want you to leave me, Jack. I don't want you to."

Jack felt his body sway like a buoy under the force of her words. He wanted to kiss her. He wanted to kiss her more than anything. He wanted to take her cool, creamy hands in his and bury his face in her copper-flecked hair. He wanted to mold his body to hers. But the ticket master was right behind them, and who knew when Emaline's mother might show up? He couldn't.

"I'll only go if I get in," he said. "And that might not happen."

She forced a smile. "With your talent? You're a shoe-in." She gripped his hand tighter, and his pulse skittered. "I'm sure of it."

Don't let go, Jack silently pleaded. *Whatever you do, Emaline, don't let go of my hand. Not yet. Please.*

She did a quick little shake of her head as if to flick away some tears and changed the subject. "By the way, do you have a date for the fall festival dance yet?" she asked.

"Only in my dreams."

"Well, I have an idea." She let her thumb slide across the back of his hand. "Why don't you ask Sarah Gelman?"

Jack's eyes grew large. "S-Sarah?"

"I think she'd love to be your date. She's crazy about you."

"I...yeah, Harry says the same thing. It's just that—"

"Jack, listen to me. I'd do anything if you and I could go together, you know that. Anything at all if we could walk arm in arm into the gymnasium and dance the night away, just the two of us."

"Me too."

"I hate it, hate it with all my heart that we can't. Still, it doesn't mean you have to stay home, does it? Come on, I'll help you pick out a corsage for Sarah. You'll pin it right here on her." She tapped Jack's chest, which flamed at her touch. "And you've already got this handsome suit. You're all set."

"Does this mean you're going to the dance with George?"

Emaline opened her mouth to speak, but a horn blast from down the track drowned her words.

They both turned to watch the steely black train speed their way. In a tumult of wind and heat, it screeched to a stop, wrapping them in a dense swirl of smoke. For a moment, the exhaust was so thick they couldn't see the ticket master behind them or the conductor in front of them. That's when they kissed. A sweet, lingering, too brief kiss. In broad daylight. With other people only yards away. For the first and the last time.

They didn't say goodbye. The train doors clanged open, and Jack simply picked up his cello and boarded the passenger car. Emaline and the skinny little dog watched as the train started out, but Jack couldn't bring himself to look back at them. He had to keep looking forward. It was the only way.

Author's Note

In a Russian village many years ago, the butcher's son was found stabbed to death on the shop floor. The butcher ran to the judge and said, "It must be a Jew! A Jew must have murdered my son and taken his blood to make Sabbath cakes."

The judge summoned the rabbi to stand trial, and since there was no evidence, he declared, "We'll settle this case the simple way. On one slip of paper, I'll write the word guilty, and the other I'll leave blank. If the rabbi draws the guilty paper, he shall burn at the stake. If he draws the blank paper, he and his people will go free."

The judge wrote guilty on both slips before placing them in a hat. But the rabbi was wise. When he drew one of the papers, he immediately popped it into his mouth and swallowed it.

"How dare you!" screamed the judge. "Now how are we to tell which paper you drew?"

"Just check the one left in the hat," answered the rabbi. He withdrew the remaining paper and showed the judge that it said guilty. "Here!" the rabbi said. "Since this one says guilty, I must have swallowed the blank one." And so the judge was forced by his own decree to free the rabbi.

Several weeks later the butcher, wracked with guilt, confessed that he himself had killed his son with a meat cleaver in a fit of rage over a lost ruble.

———

My yarn-spinning uncle told me that folktale when I was a child. I remember thinking, *thank goodness it's only a story— nothing like that ever really happens.* It never dawned on me that blood lies might exist outside of fairy tales.

Flash forward to my sophomore year of college. I was taking a sociology class called "Community Decision-Making." The professor sent us home for Thanksgiving with an assignment. Wherever we were trekking off to, we had to identify a local controversy—past or present—and write a paper about how the involved groups made their decisions.

The prof said that students usually covered Town Meeting types of issues for this assignment—water fluoridation, school budget overrides, Halloween night curfews and the like. He encouraged us to look beyond the obvious.

Off I drove to my small hometown in northern New York, thinking (a) I can't believe I have to write a paper over vacation, and (b) nothing interesting or controversial ever happens in Massena, so how am I going to come up with a topic?

I explained—rather, complained about—my predicament to my dad. He'd grown up in Massena, so I figured he'd know if anything contentious had ever come up. We sat down at our kitchen table with mugs of my mother's famous hot chocolate, and he told me, for the first time, about an extraordinary confrontation that erupted in our mild-mannered village when he was a senior in high school. It was that story which led to this book.

The incident portrayed in this novel was inspired by a real blood libel that took place when a small girl disappeared from Massena in 1928, and an innocent Jewish boy was called a murderer. The next week, after the girl was found, *The New York Times* published a letter written by American Jewish Committee president Louis Marshall to the mayor of Massena. Under the title "Reported Incident in Upstate Village is Declared First of Kind in This Country," Mr. Marshall said he was responding to "an attempt to plant on American soil the barbarous ritual murder accusation against the Jews." His letter expressed the indignation and anguish that the blood lie had caused the Jewish community.

Nothing about the incident ran in the *Massena Observer*. Although the event garnered some press at the time, it was mostly kept quiet. My purpose in writing *The Blood Lie* was to unbury this dark episode of American history. While I have imagined details and personalities, I have preserved the essence of the story. The Massena blood libel never should have happened, but it did, and the only good that can come of it is through the telling and remembering.

Five years after the blood lie in Massena, Hitler took power in Germany and began using the blood lie to justify the oppression and ultimate slaughter of the Jews. In 1937, *Der Sturmer*, a popular Nazi newspaper, even published a special ritual murder edition. Here's an excerpt:

> The carrying out of ritual murders is a law to the devout Jew...The blood of the victims is tapped by force. On

Passover, it is used in wine and matzos... The family head empties a few drops of fresh or powdered blood into the glass, wets the fingers and blesses with it everything on the table. He then exclaims, "May all Gentiles perish, as the child whose blood is contained in the bread and wine."...The Jew believes he absolves himself thus of his sins.

Although dates like 1928 and 1937 may seem like a lifetime ago, ritual murder accusations are anything but dead in the 21st century. In 2002, for instance, a student demonstration at San Francisco State University featured posters of a soup can whose label showed dripping blood, a dead baby with its stomach sliced open, and the words "Made in Israel, Palestinian children meat, slaughtered according to Jewish rites under American license." That same year, a Saudi newspaper ran an article describing how "Jewish vampires" extract the blood of teenagers to use in their Purim holiday pastries.

Shortly before Passover 2008, Russia's third largest city was plastered with posters claiming that Jews were "stealing small children and draining their blood to make their sacred bread." Also in recent years, Swedish and Canadian newspapers have published stories claiming that Jews kidnap and kill children in order to harvest and sell their internal organs.

Clearly, the blood lie is alive and well in our world. So is hatred against other groups based on their race, religion, ethnicity, disability, sexual orientation or gender identity. From cyber-bullying to violent physical attacks, vandalism to murder, oppression is out there. In 2004 alone, there were more than 9,000 reported hate offenses in the

U.S., according to the FBI. That doesn't include all the incidents that go unreported—the name-calling, exclusion, intimidation, property destruction and other offenses that people don't talk about.

I wonder if Jack Pool would be surprised at the prevalence of hate crimes today. Are you?